||||||| |||| |||||| |||||||| |||||||||||

☑ **W9-ABY-316**

Eastern   Aug 2016

Time fell off a cliff as their

Nora forgot to breathe as Reid Chamberlain's presence electrified every nerve in her body. And then he stood up without a word, crossing to her. The closer he came, the more magnetic the pull became. He was all man now—powerful in his dark gray suit, a bit rakish with his brown hair grown out long enough to curl a bit on top, and a sinfully beautiful face that became that much more devastating due to a five-o'clock shadow.

And then he was so close, she could see the gold flecks in his brown eyes that had deepened to a shade of rich mahogany. A dark, mysterious scent wafted from him, something citrusy but mixed with an exotic spice that wholly fit him. She had a feeling she'd be smelling it in her sleep tonight.

"Hi, Nora."

Reid extended his hand. For a moment, she thought he was reaching for her, to hug her, or...something. But instead, he closed the door with the heel of his hand, leaning into it, his arm brushing her shoulder.

The *snick* nearly separated her skin from her body, but she kept herself from reacting. Barely.

* * *

An Heir for the Billionaire is part of the Dynasties: The Newports series—Passion and chaos consume a Chicago real estate empire.

This item no longer belongs to Davenport Public Library

Dear Reader,

Scandal and intrigue are at the core of some of the best stories, and the Dynasties: The Newports series is no exception! I'm thrilled to introduce you to Nora Winchester, middle daughter of the powerful, abhorred Sutton Winchester. When her family discovers a previously unknown love child from Sutton's past, the ensuing inheritance drama is heartbreaking—and Nora wants nothing to do with it. She finds the perfect distraction in Reid Chamberlain, former childhood friend and current reclusive billionaire. Except he doesn't date women with kids, and Nora's son is definitely part of her full package.

I adore these lovers, especially how Nora blazed right through Reid's hang-ups, never giving the man a moment to breathe. This is the first book I've set in Chicago, and the research was so fun! I can't wait to see firsthand the places Nora and Reid visit in this book. I hope you enjoy this story and all of the others to come starring Nora's sisters, as well as some new faces.

Happy reading! Visit me online at katcantrell.com.

Kat Cantrell

DAVENPORT PUBLIC LIBRARY
321 MAIN STREET
DAVENPORT, IOWA 52801-1490

KAT CANTRELL

AN HEIR FOR
THE BILLIONAIRE

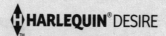

If you purchased this book without a cover you should be aware that this book is stolen property. It was reported as "unsold and destroyed" to the publisher, and neither the author nor the publisher has received any payment for this "stripped book."

Special thanks and acknowledgment are given to Kat Cantrell for her contribution to the Dynasties: The Newports miniseries

Recycling programs for this product may not exist in your area.

ISBN-13: 978-0-373-73475-7

An Heir for the Billionaire

Copyright © 2016 by Harlequin Books S.A.

All rights reserved. Except for use in any review, the reproduction or utilization of this work in whole or in part in any form by any electronic, mechanical or other means, now known or hereinafter invented, including xerography, photocopying and recording, or in any information storage or retrieval system, is forbidden without the written permission of the publisher, Harlequin Enterprises Limited, 225 Duncan Mill Road, Don Mills, Ontario M3B 3K9, Canada.

This is a work of fiction. Names, characters, places and incidents are either the product of the author's imagination or are used fictitiously, and any resemblance to actual persons, living or dead, business establishments, events or locales is entirely coincidental.

This edition published by arrangement with Harlequin Books S.A.

For questions and comments about the quality of this book, please contact us at CustomerService@Harlequin.com.

® and TM are trademarks of Harlequin Enterprises Limited or its corporate affiliates. Trademarks indicated with ® are registered in the United States Patent and Trademark Office, the Canadian Intellectual Property Office and in other countries.

Printed in U.S.A.

www.Harlequin.com

Kat Cantrell read her first Harlequin novel in third grade and has been scribbling in notebooks since then. She writes smart, sexy books with a side of sass. She's a former Harlequin So You Think You Can Write winner and an RWA Golden Heart® Award finalist. Kat, her husband and their two boys live in north Texas.

Books by Kat Cantrell

Harlequin Desire

Marriage with Benefits
The Things She Says
The Baby Deal
Pregnant by Morning
The Princess and the Player
Triplets Under the Tree
The SEAL's Secret Heirs

Happily Ever After, Inc.

Matched to a Billionaire
Matched to a Prince
Matched to Her Rival

Newlywed Games

From Ex to Eternity
From Fake to Forever

Love and Lipstick

The CEO's Little Surprise
A Pregnancy Scandal

Dynasties: The Newports

An Heir for the Billionaire

Visit her Author Profile page at Harlequin.com, or katcantrell.com, for more titles.

One

If there was any poetic justice in the world, Sutton Lazarus Winchester had gotten his.

Nora sagged back against the wall of the sterile hospital room, unable to process the inescapable fact that her seemingly infallible father was indeed dying of inoperable lung cancer. She should feel relieved. His tyrannical reign was nearly over. The man who couldn't be bothered to walk her down the aisle at her own wedding lay pale and gaunt in a hospital bed, as if a bit of his spirit had already fled for hell in advance of the rest.

The relief didn't come. Nora had traveled home to Chicago with the barest hope she might find a way to reconcile with her father in his last days. And now that she was here, the sheer difficulty of that task nearly overwhelmed her.

"I had to see it for myself," Nora murmured to her sisters, Eve and Gracie, who flanked her as she faced down their father. None of them had gotten too close to the bed in case Sutton had more gusto than he seemed to have. Right now he appeared to be asleep but that didn't matter.

Like a snake, he waited until you were within striking distance and then sank his fangs into the tenderest place he could find, injecting poison and pain until it suited him to stop. It was how he'd always operated, and Nora had no doubt he'd find a way to do it from the grave.

"We all did," Eve murmured back. "The doctor wasn't too happy with me when I asked her to allow another doctor to review the oncology reports. But I had to make sure."

Methodical to her core, Eve never missed dotting an *i* or crossing a *t*. As the oldest Winchester sister, she'd always been large and in charge and seldom let anything stand in her way.

"Wanted to see the death sentence with your own two eyes, hmm?" Nora said without malice.

Sutton had terrorized all three of his daughters, but Nora was the only one who'd grown so sick of the constant drama surrounding her father that she'd moved halfway across the country to Colorado, effectively— and gratefully—turning her back on the money, the glitter and the heartbreak of the lifestyle she'd been born into.

Eve glowered. "Wanted to make sure it wasn't manufactured. I wouldn't put it past that Newport scum to have paid off a doctor to produce a false report."

"Do you really think Carson could find someone willing to do that?" Gracie asked, and it was clear she had no ill will toward the man the sisters had recently learned was their half brother.

The total opposite of Eve, Gracie always saw the best in people. Nora's younger sister had such a big heart, even in the midst of the huge scandal caused by the recent revelation that during one of his past affairs, Sutton had fathered a son—none other than his business rival Carson Newport.

Now that Nora had seen her father, she could turn her attention to Carson, who was her second order of business while in Chicago. Oh, Nora didn't give two figs about Sutton's money and whether Carson Newport had a legal claim to any of it. Eve and Grace could fight that battle. But the man was her brother. She *was* curious about him. And she didn't appreciate the idea of her sisters losing out on their inheritance; it meant something to them, even if it came down to nothing more than a just reward for the years of being Sutton Winchester's daughters.

"I wouldn't put anything past him. There are a lot of unethical things people will gladly do for money, including doctors. And especially Newport," Eve responded, tossing her honey-blond hair over her shoulder impatiently. It was longer than Nora remembered, but then, they hadn't seen each other in quite a while. Not since before Sean had died.

The grief over her husband's untimely death, never far from the surface, bubbled up; coupled with the shock at seeing the larger-than-life head of the Winchester real estate empire laid out in a stark white hospital bed, it was too much.

One, two, three… Nora kept counting until she reached ten. That was all the time she was allowed to feel sorry for herself. Sean was gone. Nora wasn't and she had adult things to handle that wouldn't get done if she spent all her time curled up in a ball of grief as she had after the grim-faced army liaison had brought her the news that Sean had been killed in Afghanistan.

He'd never gotten to meet their son. It was the cruelest travesty in a litany of truly terrible circumstances. But Nora still had that tiny piece of her husband alive and present in their little boy, and no gun-toting terrorist could ever take that away.

A woman with thick-framed glasses and hair swept up in a no-nonsense bun appeared at Sutton's bedside, the tablet in her hand and white lab coat indicating she had medical business at hand. She checked a few things on her tablet and then glanced at the knot of Winchester women.

"I'm Dr. Wilde. We haven't met." The doctor rounded

the bed to shake Nora's hand. "You must be the nonlocal sister."

"Nora O'Malley," she affirmed. She'd shed the Winchester name as fast as she could after she and Sean tied the knot, and it would take an act of Congress to get her to ever change it to anything else. "So it's true? My father is dying and there's nothing you can do?"

Dr. Wilde bowed her head for a moment, her discreet diamond earrings sparkling in the light. "As much as I hate to admit defeat, yes. It's true. I couldn't operate, due to the tumor's location, and then the cancer spread too fast to employ chemotherapy. He probably has another five months, tops. I'm sorry."

Five months. It was way too fast. How could she find the will to forgive her father for not loving her in such a short period of time?

"Don't be," Nora insisted, even as the doctor's prognosis hit her sideways. "It's his own fault. We all told him to stop smoking but he thought that deal he'd made with the devil would keep him alive forever, I guess."

She'd known that's what the doctor would say. But it was so different to hear it from her mouth personally. That was partly the reason she'd forced herself to get on a plane to Chicago, though traveling with a two-year-old had been exhausting.

And now it was shockingly final. Sutton would be dead by New Year's Day.

Sutton's personal assistant, Valerie Smith, poked her head in the door, not one ash-blond hair out of place.

"Is your father awake yet?" she asked. "I was going to bring Declan in if you wanted."

Third order of business: to finally let her father meet his grandson.

It had been a difficult decision. The poison that Sutton managed to infuse into everybody around him couldn't be allowed to affect her son. But his grandfather was dying. Nora had hoped that on his deathbed, her father might have an epiphany about his character, his choices, his closed heart—*something* that would allow all of them to make peace with Sutton's passing and go on.

"No, he's still asleep." Nora couldn't help but feel grateful for the reprieve. She'd steeled herself for this moment of reckoning but nothing magical had happened to the disappointment and hurt inside upon seeing her father in person. "But I'll take Declan so you can have a break."

Valerie had offered to take the cranky and bored two-year-old to the cafeteria in search of Jell-O or saltine crackers, the only two things he wanted. He refused to eat the fruit snacks and banana chips Nora had shoved in her carry-on bag—the only two things he'd wanted when she'd been packing back home. Reason was not in the wheelhouse of a toddler, so holding out the packages and telling him that was the snack he'd picked hadn't worked.

The little boy popped into the room and Nora's heart lurched, as it always did when she caught sight of his curly mop of red hair. He looked like Sean, of course, and it was both a blessing and a curse to have the visual reminder of what she'd lost. "Hey, Butterbean. Did you find some Jell-O?"

Nora extracted herself from her sisters with a hand to Gracie's arm and a smile for Eve, guilt crowding into her chest that she'd opted to take the out of caring for her son instead of sitting here with her family. They'd all been by Sutton's side from the beginning, supporting each other, showing solidarity to outsiders, but Nora just…couldn't.

Declan nodded. "Jell-O."

It came out sounding more like *je-whoa*, but Nora had never had any trouble interpreting Declan-speak. The shiny machines of the hospital room caught his attention and he weaved toward the nearest one, finger outstretched. Nora scooped him up and kissed his head. "Not so fast, Mr. Curious. Have I told you the story about the cat?"

"Cat." Declan made a sound like one, except it was more of a yowl than a traditional meow. He was so funny and precious and her heart ached that his father wasn't here to see how he'd grown, how fast he learned things, how he slept with one foot stuck out from the covers—just like Sean had.

As quickly as she could, Nora bustled her son out of the hospital room before anyone saw the tear that had slipped down her face. Sean had died nearly two years ago. She should be ready to move past it. Ready to date again, find someone to ease her loneliness. But she couldn't imagine being with someone other than Sean, who had been the love of her life, the man who had thoroughly captured her heart the moment she'd met him at a football game during her junior year of college.

Seeking a quiet place to regroup, Nora spied an alcove with two chairs away from the main hospital corridor. She and Declan settled into the chairs, or she did. He sat in the opposing one for a grand total of four seconds before he squirmed to the ground and scooted around like his pants were on fire. Nora laughed.

"Problem with your diaper there, Butterbean?"

That had been Sean's nickname for the boy the moment he'd seen the ultrasound pictures she'd held up to the camera during one of their Skype calls. She'd kept the name, even after he was born, because Declan still resembled a bean when swaddled in the brown blanket Sean's mother had bought for her grandson.

Of course, Nora didn't do much swaddling these days, not with an active two-year-old.

Declan didn't answer, too preoccupied with his task of cleaning the hospital floor with his butt. Thirty more seconds and she'd use hand sanitizer on every inch of exposed skin, before he got around to sticking a random body part in his mouth. Midwest Regional was a highly acclaimed hospital, but sick people came through these halls all the time. A mother couldn't be too careful.

"Ms. Winchester?" A young hospital worker in

plain clothes stopped near Declan. Her name badge read Amanda.

"O'Malley," Nora corrected. "But yes, formerly Winchester."

And she didn't choke on it. There might be hope for her yet to work through all her anger and disillusionment with her father.

The worker smiled. "There's a private room set up for the family if you'd like me to show it to you."

"Oh, yes. Of course."

How could she have missed that Sutton's wealth and influence had extended even to the hospital? It had been a long time since Nora had lived the life of a socialite, and even longer since she'd wanted to. But the lure of a private place, away from the crowded hospital, called to her.

Amanda punched in the code on the keypad outside the room and then promised to write it down for her. Nora pushed open the door and nearly gasped, but not over the sumptuously appointed room. Her mother's house had far more antique rugs and dark, heavy furniture than this place. No, her attention was firmly on the long table lining the wall that held enough food for four Winchester families. The empty bags under the table sported the logo for Iguazu, a new, trendy Argentinian fusion restaurant so hot that Nora had even heard of it back home in Colorado. A couple of uniformed delivery people were still setting up the warming mechanisms for the silver serving trays, so the food had obviously just arrived.

"What is all this?" Nora asked Amanda.

"Someone sent it for the family. Oh—" Amanda rummaged in her pocket "—there's a note for you."

Intrigued, Nora accepted the envelope and scooped up Declan with her other arm as he eyed the blue flame under the rolltop chafing dishes. "Thank you."

Amanda wrote down the keypad code on a sticky note and cheerfully waved as she exited behind the delivery people. Nora sat in one of the overstuffed wingback chairs and wedged Declan in tight so he couldn't squirm away, then ripped open the envelope.

The typed note was short and to the point: *Good food can make anything more bearable.*

In closing, the note contained only a simple statement— *Cordially Yours.* No signature.

Nora's eyes narrowed as she read over the phrase again. It tickled the edges of her memory and then came to her all at once. It was a phrase that had been a bit of a joke between Nora and a friend—Reid Chamberlain.

Wow. That was a name Nora hadn't thought about in years. Reid, his brother, Nash, and his sister, Sophia, had gone to the same private schools as the Winchester girls, practically since birth. Reid and Nora were the same age and had often been in the same class. Their parents ran in the elite circles of Chicago society, so it was only natural that they'd seen each other socially, and at boring grown-up events. What else was there for kids to do but bond?

It would have made more sense for Nora to become

friends with Sophia, but it hadn't happened that way. Reid had always been the object of her fascination.

They'd spent a good bit of time getting into trouble together, playing make-believe in the cupboards of each other's kitchens until the servants chased them out, or getting up a game of hide-and-seek across the expansive Chamberlain estate grounds with their siblings. She'd loved it when they hid in the branches of the same tree, giggling quietly behind their hands when Nash or Gracie stood directly below, frustrated over not being able to find them. For a while, she'd had a bit of a crush on Reid.

But that had been before he grew into his looks and body, both of which put him firmly in the sights of every teenaged socialite-in-training in the greater Chicago area, shoving Nora to the back of the pack. Then Reid had started running with a crowd that worshipped at the altar of money, prestige and fast cars. She didn't blame him. Ninety-nine percent of the people in her life subscribed to the philosophy of *whoever has the most toys at the end wins*. They'd grown apart. It happened.

Last she'd heard, Reid Chamberlain had only increased his wealth and prestige through a series of brilliant moves in the hotel industry. He dominated the Chicago market along with a host of other cities.

Surely Reid wasn't the one who'd sent the smorgasbord. They hadn't talked in years and the joke involving *cordially yours* hadn't been a code of any sort, just something they'd said to each other when they mimicked how grown-ups talked when trying to impress other grown-ups. Lots of people could use the phrase on a regular basis.

Nora texted Eve and in a few moments, the rest of the Winchesters barreled into the private room to see the anonymous gift for themselves. Since she hadn't eaten in forever, Nora fixed a plate for Declan with a few French fries, his favorite and likely the only thing from the table he'd eat, and then took full advantage of the generosity of their unknown benefactor for herself. The dishes held layers and layers of steaming, mouthwatering food: Argentinian asado-style steak thick with chimichurri sauce, a tray of empanadas, a variety of grilled vegetables and cheeses.

Nora took a bit of everything, intending to go back for more of the dishes she liked the best. Eve and Gracie followed suit as they chatted about the identity of their anonymous friend, but even after a round of seconds, the spread looked like it had barely been touched.

"This food is delicious," Nora commented. "But it won't last long and there's so much of it. We should share it with the staff."

"That's a great idea," Gracie said enthusiastically. "They all work so hard. I wonder how often any of them get to eat at a place like Iguazu, where you have to know someone to get a table. I've only been there once and that took some doing. I'll mention it to Amanda so she can spread the word."

You needed an "in" to eat at Iguazu? Nora's intrigue

meter shot into the red. Who would have sent food to the Winchester family from such an exclusive place? One of Sutton's associates? People tolerated Sutton because he was powerful, and sure, lots of them had sent impersonal gifts over the years, but rarely did anyone go out of their way to do something difficult or thoughtful. Even more impressed with the gesture, Nora fingered the note in her pocket.

Nurses, doctors and hospital staff streamed into the room in short order, exclaiming over the feast and thanking the Winchester women for their generosity. Crowd noise increased as people found seats and socialized. Nora's temples started to pound as the long day of travel caught up with her.

On the other side of the room, Declan had climbed into Gracie's lap, and she laughed as he stole French fries off her plate, apparently not having stuffed his little face enough with those his mother had given him. Declan was in good hands with his aunt, providing Nora with the perfect opportunity to grab a few minutes to herself.

Nora caught Gracie's eye and nodded to the door, then held up her palm with her fingers spread, mouthing, "Five minutes?"

Gracie smiled and waved her off.

Gratefully, Nora ducked out and went to the ladies' room to splash some water on her face. Belatedly, she realized there was probably a private bathroom in the area she'd just left. It had been a while since Nora had lived in her family's wealthy orbit. She'd never really embraced the privileged lifestyle anyway, even choosing to go to the University of Michigan, a public college, much to her mother's chagrin. But that was where she'd met Sean, so she'd considered it fate.

Out of nowhere, Reid popped into her head again. He'd gone to Yale, if she recalled correctly. Not that she'd spent a lot of time keeping track of him, but the private high school they'd attended had been small enough that everyone knew everyone else's business.

As she fingered the note in her pocket again, Nora's curiosity got the best of her. What if Reid had sent the catered spread? She should thank him. Gracie and Eve had known Reid, of course, but they'd never been close with any of the Chamberlain siblings, not as Nora had.

But why would Reid have done something so nice without signing the note? Suddenly, she had to know if her childhood friend had been behind the gesture. If for no other reason than to satisfy her curiosity.

Nora was nothing if not resourceful. After all, she'd walked away from her family's money and lived a simple life in Colorado on the monthly Dependent Indemnity Compensation payment that the government sent Nora as a surviving spouse of a military serviceman killed in the line of duty. Creativity came with the territory.

She pulled out her phone and tapped up the restaurant's website, then called. A cultured female voice answered. "Iguazu. How may I help you?"

"This is…Ms. O'Malley from Mr. Chamberlain's office." Nora crossed her fingers. She hated lying, but the ends justified this little white one. "Mr. Chamberlain would like confirmation that the food he ordered to be delivered to the Winchester family at Midwest Regional was delivered."

"Absolutely, let me verify."

Music piped through the speakers as Nora was put on hold. She grinned. That had been way too easy.

The music cut off as the Iguazu employee came back on the line. "Ms. O'Malley? Yes, the food was delivered and as specified, the note given directly to Nora Winchester. Please let Mr. Chamberlain know we're pleased he's chosen Iguazu for his catering needs and we look forward to his next event."

Somehow Nora squeaked out a "Thank you," though how she'd spoken when her tongue had gone completely numb, she'd never know.

Reid had not only sent the food, he'd specified that *she* should receive the note? Why? The signature *had* been some kind of code. One he'd clearly thought would mean something to her. And it did. She'd been besieged by memories of an easier time, before Sean, before she'd really understood what an SOB her father was.

Reid had wanted her to figure it out. She had to know why.

After the long trip and the blow of seeing her father so ill in that hospital bed, yet not feeling the rush of forgiveness she'd hoped for, Nora should have *wanted* to go home and shut out the world. But she'd been doing that for two years and all it had gotten her was a severe case of loneliness and a crushing sense of vulnerability.

Very little had happened lately that she'd had any control over. Her life had been spinning without her permission and all she'd been able to do was hang on. It was time to do something affirmative. Something decisive. Like thank an old friend for his kindness.

Two

On the way to Reid Chamberlain's downtown Chicago office, Nora pulled up a few articles about him on her phone. If she was going to beard the man in his den, she should at least know a few things about who he'd become over the years.

Gracie had volunteered to take Declan back to the Winchester estate, where Nora would be staying while in Chicago, and then insisted on calling for a car to take Nora on her mysterious errand. Being secretive wasn't second nature to Nora, but she didn't want to bring up Reid, at least not until she knew the purpose behind his kind gesture.

Especially when all of the articles she'd managed to find about Reid pointed to a very different person from what she'd expected. There were almost no pictures of him, save one very grainy shot that showed Reid rushing from a dark car to the covered doorway of one of his hotels. He'd turned his face from the camera, so the angle showed only his profile, but even that little bit clearly conveyed his annoyance at the photographer.

The caption underneath read "Reclusive billionaire Reid Chamberlain."

Reclusive? *Reid?* He'd been the life of the party as long as Nora could remember. Heck, that was the reason they'd grown apart—he'd become so popular, his time was in constant demand.

Doubly intrigued, Nora glanced up as the car slowed to a stop and the uniformed driver slid out to open the back door for her to exit. She got out and found herself standing in front of the brand-new Metropol Hotel in the heart of downtown Chicago.

A study in glass and steel, the hotel towered over her, reaching to the heavens. *Good grief.* This was Reid's office? She'd read that Nash Chamberlain had designed the Metropol, and it was nothing short of breathtaking, rising several dozen stories high and twisting every so often. The architectural know-how required to design it must have been great, indeed.

Impressed, Nora swept through the door opened by a uniformed attendant and approached the concierge, glad she'd opted for heels and a classic summer-weight pantsuit today. The concierge glanced up with a ready smile. Her mind went blank. Lying to the woman from

Iguazu had been one thing, but this man was right in front of her, staring at her expectantly. She should have thought this through.

What if Reid wasn't here? Or hadn't really wanted her to seek him out? She'd only assumed he'd meant for her to figure it out. He might actually be mad that she'd tracked him down.

So what if he was mad. This trek had been about something greater than a mere thank-you. *Taking control here.* Nora squared her shoulders. No apologies.

"I'm here to see Mr. Chamberlain. Tell him Nora O…Winchester is here." And she didn't even choke on the name. "Nora Winchester. He'll see me right away."

Wow. *Brazen* should be her middle name. The articles had called Reid reclusive and she'd waltzed right in to demand that he admit her without question? This was a dumb idea.

The concierge nodded. "Of course, Ms. Winchester. He's expecting you."

Nora picked her jaw up off the floor for the second time that day. "Thank you."

The concierge tapped a bell and a young man in a discreet rust-colored uniform that mirrored the hotel's accents appeared by Nora's side before she could fully process that Reid was *expecting her.*

"William will show you to the elevators and ensure that you reach Mr. Chamberlain's office," the concierge said.

Meekly, she followed the bellhop to the elevator

bank, her heels sinking into the plush carpet that covered the rich dark hardwood floors. When they got on the elevator, the bellhop swiped a badge over the reader above the buttons and pushed one for the forty-seventh floor.

"Forty-seven and forty-eight are secure floors," William explained with a smile. "Only VIPs get to see Mr. Chamberlain. It's been quite a while since we've had one."

VIPs only. And Nora Winchester was one. What would have happened if she'd introduced herself as Nora O'Malley? Would the concierge have politely booted her out the door?

Nervous all at once, she discreetly checked her hair and makeup in the mirrored paneling of the elevator. She'd twisted her blond hair up in a chignon this morning before her flight, and several loose strands had corkscrewed around her face. Not a bad look.

Silly. What did it matter how she looked? Reid had thrown her all off-kilter by telling his staff to expect her.

The elevator dinged and within moments William was ushering her into a reception area populated by a stately woman with steel-colored hair, who closed her laptop instantly as Nora entered.

"You must be Ms. Winchester," she said. "Mr. Chamberlain asked for you to be shown right in."

Far too quickly, the receptionist steered her through a set of glass doors and to an open entryway at the end of the hall, then discreetly melted away.

The man behind the wide glass desk glanced up the moment Nora walked across the threshold of his office.

Time fell off a cliff as their eyes locked.

Nora forgot to breathe as Reid Chamberlain's presence electrified every nerve in her body. And then he stood without a word, crossing to her. The closer he came, the more magnetic the pull became. He was all man now—powerful in his dark gray suit, a bit rakish with his brown hair grown out long enough to curl a bit on top, and sinfully beautiful, with a face that became that much more devastating due to a five o'clock shadow that darkened his jaw.

And then he was so close she could see the gold flecks in his brown eyes. A dark, mysterious scent wafted from him, something citrusy but mixed with an exotic spice that wholly fit him. She had a feeling she'd be smelling it in her sleep that night.

"Hi, Nora."

Reid extended his hand. For a moment, she thought he was reaching for her, to hug her, or…something. But instead, he closed the door and leaned into it, his arm brushing her shoulder.

The *snick* of the door nearly made her jump out of her skin, but she kept herself from reacting. Barely. Did he have something in mind that was so intimate and private that it wasn't fit for prying eyes?

Her pulse jumped into her throat. "Hi, Reid."

He crossed his arms and contemplated her. "You got the note."

"Yes." Impulsively, she put out her palm, intending to touch Reid on the arm to express her thanks.

But at the last minute, something in his expression stopped her. Something dangerous, with an edge she didn't understand, but wanted to. Touching him suddenly held all kinds of nonverbal implications, maybe even an invitation she wasn't sure she meant to extend.

Goodness. How had a simple thank-you become so... *charged*? She let her hand drop to her side and his gaze followed it, marking the action.

"What can I do for you?" he asked simply.

He was not the same boy she remembered. She could see hints of his teenage self in the way he held his body, and small things such as the length of his lashes were the same, but his gaze had grown hard and opaque. It was almost as if he'd grown an extra layer between himself and the rest of the world and no one was allowed to breach it. One of the things she'd always liked about Reid Chamberlain was his smile. And that was noticeably absent.

The man was—according to the news articles—reclusive, and wealthier than King Solomon, Croesus and Bill Gates put together. But it didn't seem to have made him happy.

What could he do for her, indeed? Probably not much. But maybe she could do something for him. "You can smile for me, Reid. It might actually break this awkward tension."

* * *

Against all odds, the corners of Reid's mouth twitched. He fought to suppress the smile because he didn't want to encourage Nora Winchester into thinking she could command him into doing her will five minutes into their renewed acquaintance.

Besides, Reid didn't smile. That was for people who had a lightness of spirit that allowed for such a thing. He didn't. Normally. Nora had barreled into his office and the moment he'd seen her, it was like a throwback to another time and place—before all the shadows had seeped into his soul.

Which sounded overly dramatic, even to himself. That was why he never thought about his own miserable existence and instead worked eighteen hours a day so he could fall into bed exhausted at the end of it. When you slept like the dead, you didn't dream. You didn't lie awake questioning all the choices you'd made and cursing the genetics that prevented you from doing a simple thing like becoming a father to your orphaned niece and nephew.

Nora's presence shouldn't have changed anything. But it had. She'd breathed life into his office that hadn't been there a moment ago and he was having a hard time knowing what to do with it.

It was troubling enough that she'd tracked him down in the first place. And more troubling still that he'd been anticipating her arrival in a way that he hadn't *anticipated* anything in a long while.

"Smiling is for politicians and people with agendas," he finally said.

The air remained thick with tension and something else he wasn't in a hurry to dispel—awareness. On both sides. Nora was just as intrigued by him as he was by her. Reid was nothing if not well versed in reading his opposition. And in his world, everyone was the opposition, even Nora Winchester, a woman he hadn't spoken to in nearly fifteen years and who'd apparently interpreted his note as an invitation to invade his privacy.

He should be annoyed. He wasn't. That made Nora dangerous and unpredictable. Unexpectedly, it added to her intrigue. The heavy pull between them tingled along his muscles, heating him to the point of discomfort. He hadn't been this affected by a woman's presence since he was a teenager.

"Oh, really. And you don't have an agenda?" Nora crossed her arms in an exaggerated pose he suspected was designed to mimic his. "What was with the note, then?"

"It's polite to include a note with a gift," he replied as he fought a smile for the second time. He hadn't expected to like the grown-up version of Nora as much as he did. What was he supposed to do with her?

When his admin had called Iguazu to check on the delivery, imagine his surprise to learn that a mystery woman from "his office" had already called. A quick check-in with the hospital told him that Nora had indeed received his note. It hadn't taken much to guess she'd figured out that he'd sent the catering and would be along to see him in short order. He'd been right.

"Uh-huh. And is it customary to use a private joke in said note and then pretend you didn't intend for me to figure out you sent it?"

Her wide, beautiful mouth tipped up at the corners and communicated far more than her words did. She was toying with him. Maybe even *flirting*. Women didn't flirt with him as a rule. Usually they were much more direct, wrangling introductions from mutual acquaintances and issuing invitations into their beds before he'd learned their last names.

He'd taken a few of them up on it. He wasn't a monk. But he'd never held a conversation with one or called one again. Not since the day when his father had killed more than half of his family, including himself.

Nora was a first. In more ways than one. His body's awareness dialed up a notch. She was close enough to touch but he didn't reach out. Not yet. Not until he got a much better handle on his reaction to her. And maybe not even then. Nora certainly hadn't dropped by to be seduced by the CEO of Chamberlain Group. But that didn't automatically mean she'd be averse to the idea. It just meant he needed a clearer sense of the lay of the land before he made a move on a childhood friend.

"Are you…*accusing* me of deliberately trying to get your attention with a throwaway signature line on a note?" Reid hadn't enjoyed interaction with a woman this much in so long, he couldn't even *say* how long.

Her gaze narrowed. "Are you denying it?"

Cordially Yours. He hadn't uttered that phrase in over a decade. How had she remembered that joke? Or maybe a better question was: why had he put it in the note?

Maybe he'd intended for this to go down exactly as it had.

When he'd heard about Sutton Winchester's terminal diagnosis, Reid's first thought had been of Nora. They hadn't spoken in a long time, but she'd played an important role in his youth, namely that of a confidante for a boy trying to navigate a difficult relationship with his parents. He remembered Nora Winchester fondly and had never even said thank you for the years of distraction she'd provided, both at school and at parties.

The gift had been about balancing the scales. Reid didn't like owing anyone anything.

He certainly hadn't sent the food for Winchester's benefit. The old man could—and most definitely would—rot in hell before Reid would lift a finger to help him. The man had more shady business deals and crooked politicians in his back pocket than a shark had teeth. Reid wouldn't soon forget how Chamberlain Group had been on the receiving end of a personal screw-over, courtesy of Sutton Winchester.

"The food was for old time's sake. Nothing more." Nor should he pretend it was anything more. "Let's just say I wasn't expecting a personal thank-you for the catering, and leave it at that."

She laughed and it slid down his spine, unleashing

a torrent of memories. Nora *was* an old friend, and for a man who didn't have many, it suddenly meant something to him that he had a history with this woman. A positive history. She'd known his sister, Sophia, and that alone made her different from anyone else in his life except Nash.

Yeah, letting her walk away untouched wasn't happening. Reid had long ago accepted his selfish nature and he wanted more of Nora's laugh.

"Obviously you *were* expecting me." Nora's gaze raked over his body as she called him on it. "Your staff couldn't have been clearer that they'd been waiting for me to arrive. How did you guess I'd be coming by?"

"Oddly enough, you tipped me off. My admin called Iguazu and learned that Ms. O'Malley from my office had already inquired after the status of the delivery."

Guilt clouded Nora's gaze and she shifted her eyes to the right, staring at a spot near his shoulder. "Well, you didn't sign the note. How else was I supposed to figure out if you were the one behind the nice gesture?"

"I don't make nice gestures," he corrected her. "And you weren't supposed to figure it out. Is Ms. O'Malley a fake name you use often to perform nefarious deeds?"

He couldn't resist teasing her when it was so obvious she hadn't a deceptive bone in her body. Flirting, teasing and smiling—or nearly doing so anyway—were all things he hadn't indulged in for a very long time, and all things he'd like to continue doing.

But only with Nora. All at once, he was glad she'd tracked him down.

"Yes," she informed him pertly. "It's a name I use often for all my deeds. I got married."

Genuine disappointment lanced through his gut. Where had that come from? Had he really been entertaining a notion of backing Nora up against the door and taking that wide mouth under his seriously enough that learning she was married would affect him so greatly?

Ridiculous. He shouldn't be thinking of her that way at all. She was an old friend who would soon walk out of his life, never to be heard from again. It was better that way. It hardly mattered whether she'd gotten married. Of course she had. A woman as stunningly beautiful and intrinsically kind as Nora Winchester wouldn't stay single.

Some of the sensual tension faded a bit. But not all. Nora's smile did interesting things to him and he didn't think he could put a halt to it if he tried.

"Belated congratulations," he offered smoothly. "I hadn't heard."

"You wouldn't have. Sean was stationed out of Fort Carson in Colorado. We got married on base, much to my mother's dismay. It was a small ceremony and it happened nearly seven years ago." She waved it off. "Ancient history. I'm a widow now, anyway."

"I'm sorry for your loss." The phrase came automatically, as he did still have a modicum of manners despite not spending much time in polite company.

But Nora—a *widow*? Dumbfounded, he zeroed in on Nora's face, seeking…something, but he had no idea what. She'd said it so matter-of-factly, as if she'd grieved and moved on. How had she done that? If it was so easy, Reid would have done the same.

The specters of Sophia and his mother still haunted him, which didn't mix well with polite company, and he doubted he'd ever be able to toss off the information that they'd passed as calmly as Nora had just informed him that her husband had died.

Death was a painful piece of his past that shouldn't be the thing he had in common with Nora. The loss of his mother and sister *should* be the reason he showed Nora the door. Nonetheless, it instantly bonded them in a way that their shared history hadn't. He wanted to explore that more. See what this breath of fresh air might do to chase away the dark, oily shadows inside, even for a few moments.

"Thank you," she said with a nod. "For the condolences and the food. I want to thank you properly, though. Maybe spend some time catching up. I'd like to hear what you've been up to. Let me take you to dinner."

That bordered on the worst idea ever conceived. He cultivated a reputation for being a loner with practiced ease, and didn't want to expose their new rapport to prying eyes. And there would be plenty if he took a woman to dinner in a small town like Chicago.

"I don't go out in public. Why don't you come back

for dinner here? I live in the penthouse, one floor up. My private chef is the best in the business."

No, *that* was the worst idea ever conceived. Nora, behind closed doors. Laughing, flirting… It didn't take much to imagine where that would lead. He'd have her in his arms before the main course, hoping to find the secrets deep in Nora's soul. Especially the one that led to moving past tragedy and pain.

But the invitation was already out and he wasn't sorry he'd issued it. Though he might be before the evening was out. No one had ever crossed the threshold of his home except very select staff members who were well paid to keep their mouths shut about their boss's private domain.

That didn't stop the rampant speculation about what went on in his "lair," as he'd been told it was called. Some went so far as to guess that all sorts of illicit activity went on behind closed doors, as if he'd built some kind of pleasure den and had lured innocent young girls into his debauchery.

The truth was much darker. Racked with guilt over not being able to save his mother and Sophia, he wasn't fit for public consumption and the best way to avoid people was to stay home.

The distance he maintained between himself and the rest of the world was what kept him sane. Other people didn't get that part of his soul was missing, never to be recovered. The hole inside had been filled with a blackness he couldn't exorcise and sometimes, it bubbled up to the surface like thick, dark oil that coated everything in its path. Other people didn't understand that. And he didn't want to explain it to them.

"You don't go out in public?" Curiosity lit up her gaze. "I read that you were reclusive. I thought they were exaggerating. You being all shut up away from other people doesn't jibe with the person I once knew."

"Things change," he countered roughly. "I have a lot of money and power. People generally want a piece of both. It's easier to stay away from the masses."

His standard answer. Everyone bought it.

"Sounds very lonely." Somehow, she'd moved closer, though he hadn't thought they were all that far apart in the first place. Her wide smile warmed him in places he'd forgotten existed. Places better left out of this equation.

"Expedient." He cleared his throat. "I run a billion-dollar empire here. Not much time for socializing."

"Yet your first instinct was an invitation to dinner. Seems like you're reaching out to me."

Their gazes caught. Held. A wealth of unspoken messages zipped between them but hell if he knew what was being said. What he wanted to say.

"It's just dinner," he countered and he could tell by her expression that she didn't believe the lie any more than he did. They both knew it would be more. Maybe just a rekindling of their friendship, which felt necessary all of a sudden. Nora was someone from before his life had turned into the twisted semblance of normal that it had become.

"Oh, come on, Reid." She laughed again. "We're both adults now. After the note and the rather obvious way you shut the door half a second after I walked through it, I think it's permissible to call it a date."

He glanced at the closed office door and just as he was about to explain that he valued his privacy—nothing more—he discovered his mouth had already curved up in a ghost of a smile, totally against his will. "A date, then."

Yet another first. Reid Chamberlain didn't date. At least not since his father had murdered the most important people in Reid's life—and Reid had been forced to reconcile that he shared a genetic bond with a monster.

Three

The dress Nora had chosen for her date with Reid—or rather the dress Eve and Gracie had bullied her into wearing—should've been be illegal.

Actually, if she moved the wrong way, it would be.

The plunging neckline hit a point well below her breasts and the fabric clung to every curve Nora had forgotten she had. Simple and black, it was more than a cocktail dress. It was a dress that said: *I'm here for what comes after dinner.*

Nora was not okay with that message. Or maybe she was. *No.* She wasn't.

"I can't wear this," she mumbled again.

"You can and you are," Eve countered. Again. "I've only worn it one time. No one will recognize it."

As if committing a fashion faux pas was the most troublesome aspect of this situation.

Part of the problem was that Nora liked the way she looked in the dress. The other part of the problem was that Nora didn't have the luxury of sticking around for what came after dinner, if she even had a mind to be available for...*that*. She had Declan. Her son made everything ten times more complicated, even what should have been a simple dinner with an old friend.

A friend whose very gaze had touched places inside her that she hadn't known existed. Until now, she hadn't realized how very good it felt to be the object of a man's interest. Sean had loved her and of course had paid attention to her, but this was something else. Something with a tinge of wicked. Purely sexual. It was exhilarating and frightening at the same time.

She practiced walking in front of the full-length mirror affixed to the closet in the master suite of her father's guesthouse. Yep. If she stumbled, her bare nipples would peek out with a big ole hello. So she wouldn't stumble.

Eve fastened a jewel-encrusted drop necklace around Nora's neck. "Perfect. It draws attention exactly where it should. To your neckline."

"It's like a big arrow that points to my boobs." Nora tried to shorten the chain but Eve took the necklace out of her hands and let the stone fall back into place in the valley between her breasts.

"Yes. This is not a date with a guy you met at

church," Eve advised her. "Reid Chamberlain has a well-earned reputation. He doesn't invite women into his private domain. What few he's spent time with are very hush-hush about it, and it doesn't take a rocket scientist to figure out that he's giving these women a ride worth keeping their mouths shut over. You are beautiful and have something to offer. Make him aware of it and then make him work for it."

Gracie nodded as Nora swallowed. "It's not like that. We're old friends."

Eve took a flatiron from the vanity to their right and fussed a bit more with Nora's hair. "Yeah, well, I've known Reid a long time and he's never asked me to dinner."

Eve and Reid hadn't been friends, though.

Nora's history with Reid gave her one up on all these other women whom he *hadn't* asked on a date. When Nora had labeled it as such, she'd hoped that would dispel some of the confusion. It was always better to call a spade a spade, and it was clear—to her at least—that there was something simmering between herself and Reid. And dinner was A Date, she had no doubt.

Nora didn't date. She hadn't dated anyone since she'd met Sean nearly ten years ago. The only reason she had even agreed to this one was because Reid was a friend. It afforded her a measure of comfort to think about jumping back into the pool with someone she knew. Someone she'd always had a crush on.

Except the way he looked at her… She shivered.

There was a lot more than friendship in his dark, enigmatic gaze. Tonight was a chance to finally see what it was like to be with Reid and not think of him as "just" a friend. The real question was whether she'd act on the undercurrents or chicken out. Nora hadn't had sex in over two years. What if she'd forgotten how?

"Reid is not some mysterious guy with a shady reputation," Nora insisted, but it was mostly to convince herself.

He *was* different. She'd definitely noticed that earlier today. Darker, more layered. But she'd gotten the distinct impression he needed to connect with someone—*her*. Perhaps for the same reason she'd agreed to the date in the first place. They had a history. Being in his presence today had brought back some good memories. No reason that couldn't continue.

"Nora, honey, you've been away from Chicago for a long time." Eve wrangled the same lock of hair until she got it the way she wanted it. "Trust me, I've crossed paths with him a few times now that I'm taking a more active role in the inner workings of Elite. He was short with me, all business. He's like that with everyone. Except you, I guess."

"He runs a billion-dollar company," Nora said faintly. "You of all people should know that means you can't be Mr. Pushover, especially not in meetings."

Gracie shook her head and added, "Just be careful. The girl who does my nails is convinced he pays off the women he dates. Word is that he's got some very unusual…tastes. Things he prefers in the bedroom. Things that are not fit to be discussed among polite company. That's why they never talk about it. They're well paid to keep quiet and probably don't want anyone to know they participated."

"That's just speculation," Nora scoffed as her pulse jumped.

What kind of things? Unfortunately, she had a good enough imagination and some of what she envisioned couldn't be unseen. It was a delicious panorama of poses, featuring Reid Chamberlain in splendorous, naked glory. Not that she'd ever seen him without clothes, but Reid was devastating and gorgeous in a suit. It wasn't a stretch to assume he'd look good out of one, too. Throw in this new dark and mysterious side? It only added to his appeal. And heightened her nerves.

"Besides, it's dinner between old friends," Nora continued, her voice growing stronger as her resolve solidified. Whatever his predilections were in the bedroom, she'd probably never find out. "That's all. I'm a mom. We don't incite men's fantasies."

And she had to keep Declan forefront in her thoughts. There were no grown-up sleepovers in her future, not when she had a two-year-old who still woke up calling for mama in the middle of the night. This was a thank-you dinner, nothing more. An escape from her father's scary health problems and the scandal of the inheritance drama.

Eve's brows quirked as she spun Nora to face the

mirror. "Honey, that body is every inch a man's fantasy, and by the way, you're a strong, entertaining woman. A man can and will be as attracted to what's up here—" she tapped Nora's temple "—as by what's down here."

All three Winchester sisters followed Eve's gesture as she indicated Nora's torso. Even Nora couldn't argue that the dress did highlight her curves. Nor could she argue that any man who was worth her time would be attracted to her brain.

"Regardless, I'll be home by ten," Nora promised. "Ten thirty at the latest."

She kissed Declan and left him in Gracie's capable hands. They settled in to watch cartoons, waving to Nora as she left, nervous as ever.

On the way over to the Metropol, Nora sat ramrod straight in her seat, too edgy to relax. The driver didn't try to talk to her, which was a blessing.

Her imagination went into overdrive again. If Reid did have unusual tastes…did that automatically mean she'd say no? The thought of being a bit more adventurous than normal with someone she trusted got her a little hot and bothered. Because of course Reid was still Reid. There was nothing anyone could say to convince her that he'd turned into a monster who incited women into submitting to his twisted sexual practices.

Besides, her heart belonged to Sean. Anything that took place with Reid could be left behind once she went home to Colorado. It was freeing to not have the slightest worry about what might happen in the future.

When the concierge snapped for a bellboy to escort her to the penthouse—a different bellboy from last time—she forgot to breathe for a moment as the elevator doors slid shut. This was a one-way ticket to something she had no idea if she was *really* ready for.

You're being silly. You have no idea if the rumors are true. No idea if Reid even planned to do anything more than eat dinner. Also? He wasn't going to hold her prisoner. If she didn't like where the evening was headed, all she had to do was leave.

Of course, there was always the possibility that she would be on board with more than dinner. Maybe. The jury was still out.

The elevator doors parted, leading to a small alcove with a dazzling white marble floor. She stepped out and faced a closed unmarked door directly opposite the elevator.

"Have a good night, ma'am." With a silent swoosh of the elevator doors, the bellhop disappeared and then there was nothing left to do but knock.

Except the door opened before she could. Reid stood on the other side, wearing a different suit from earlier. This one had more closely cut lines and a darker hue and showcased his broad shoulders in a way she couldn't quite ignore. His jaw was shadowed with stubble that lent his handsome face a dangerous edge. Or perhaps she was imagining the edge after her conversation with Grace and Eve.

"Hi, Reid." Her voice came out all breathless and

excited, turning the short phrase into something else entirely.

His gaze slowly traveled down her length, stopping every so often as if he'd run across something worthy of further examination. She felt the heat rise in her exposed chest but she refused to cover herself by crossing her arms. Still, her muscles flexed to do exactly that three times in a row.

"That dress was worth waiting for," he finally said, his voice as smooth as it had been earlier.

"Waiting for?" She scowled to cover her excitement. Two seconds in and he was already starting the seduction part of the evening, was he? "I wasn't late. I'm right on time."

His dark eyes took on a tinge of amusement, but his smile still hadn't returned. "By my count, I've been waiting fifteen years."

Oh, my. She fell into the possibilities of that statement with a big splat. Had he harbored secret feelings for her way back, as she had for him?

That couldn't be what he meant. He hadn't exactly been sitting around pining over her. "What are you talking about? You forgot I existed the second you turned sixteen and your parents gave you that Porsche for your birthday."

He crossed his arms and leaned on the door frame. "Would you like to continue this argument over a drink, or stay in the hall?"

"You haven't invited me in yet."

"I was busy."

He gave her another sweeping once-over that pulled at her core. And still, he didn't step aside to allow her to enter his private domain.

She could not get a handle on him, and only part of that stemmed from her sisters' warnings swirling around in the back of her mind. He'd invited her here, yet didn't seem to know what to do with her. Maybe she should help him out.

"Well, I'm thirsty," she informed him with a touch of frost. "So I choose the drink over the hall. You must not entertain much or you'd have already poured me a glass of wine."

A ghost of a smile played at his lips. "Forgive me, then. I *don't* entertain often and my manners are atrocious. Please come in, Ms. O'Malley."

With that, he stepped aside and swept his hand out. Clearly, she was supposed to take it. So she did.

The moment their flesh connected, awareness sizzled across her skin, raising goose bumps. A bit overwhelmed, she let him lead her into his penthouse.

With a whisper, the door shut behind her, closing her off from the world. And then she saw Chicago lit for the night beyond the glass wall at the edge of Reid's enormous living room.

"Oh," she gasped and his hand tightened on hers. "That's an amazing view."

Neon and stars, glass and steel, as far as the eye

could see. The world was still out there, but they were insulated from it up here, high above the masses.

"I totally agree," he said quietly and she glanced at him.

His gaze, hot and heavy, was locked on her. Unblinking. Unsettling.

"You're not even looking." And then she realized what he meant and heat flushed her nearly exposed breasts again. "Um, didn't you promise me a drink?"

"I did. Come with me."

Apparently loath to let go of her hand, he led her to a wet bar where an uncorked bottle of wine stood next to two wineglasses. From that vantage point, she could see into the dining room, where a long table was set for two.

"Your servants have been busy," she commented as he finally dropped her hand to pour the red wine, filling each glass far past the line she'd have said would be an acceptable amount for a lightweight drinker such as herself.

But then, Reid didn't really know that about her.

"I gave my servants the night off." He handed her a glass and when she took it, he held his up in a quick toast. "To old friends."

She nodded and tossed back a healthy swallow. How she got the wine down her throat was beyond her; he hadn't taken his eyes off her once since she'd walked through the door and her self-consciousness was so thick you could cut it with a knife.

They were alone in this penthouse where no one

could enter unless they had a special key for the elevator. Blessedly, deliciously *alone*. Should she be frightened? She wasn't.

Reid had gone to some trouble in anticipation of her arrival. The ambiance was sensual, edgy and quite delicious. All hard things to come by as a widowed single mom. Maybe she was far more wicked than she should be, but Reid made her feel beautiful and desirable and she wasn't going to apologize for liking it.

"Tell me something," she said impulsively, suddenly interested in picking up the thread of their conversation from the hallway. "You said you'd been waiting fifteen years for me to show up. What did you mean?"

He cocked his head, tossing a few curls into disarray, and she liked that he wasn't one of those men who used a ton of hair products. She could slide her fingers through his hair easily.

The thought warmed her further. That would be bold, indeed, if she just reached out and touched him. But that didn't mean she couldn't—or wouldn't—do it.

"Our friendship means something to me. I…didn't ever tell you that."

"Oh." A bit thunderstruck, she stared at him as the lines around his mouth grew deeper, expressing more than what his words had. Was he disappointed that he'd never told her for some reason? "That's okay, Reid. We developed other friendships and went on."

"You did. I didn't."

His cryptic words perplexed her. "You mean you

didn't make other friends? But you were always with the popular crowd, piling into each other's cars after school and leaving dances or football games together to go someplace more exciting. Or at least that's always how I imagined it."

Reid shrugged slightly. "I passed the time with them. That's all."

Things weren't as they appeared back when they'd been in high school? Her heart turned over with a squish. "Sounds like you were a recluse in training, even then."

If things weren't as they appeared back then, what's to say the same wasn't true now?

His expression darkened. "In a way. I've never had much luck connecting with people."

"Except me."

Bold. But she didn't take it back. They'd been dancing around each other and she wanted to get on with the evening, whatever that entailed.

Their gazes met and he watched her as he sipped his wine, neither confirming nor denying the statement.

Go bold or go home. It was her new mantra, one she wanted to embrace all at once.

"Is that why you invited me to dinner?" she asked with a small smile. "Because you're lonely?"

"There's a difference between being lonely and desiring to be alone," Reid countered.

"That doesn't really answer my question, now does it?"

Nora was so close, Reid could easily count the individual strands of hair—honey wheat, warm sand, a few shoots of platinum—draped over her shoulder. He suspected it would be cool to the touch if he slid a strand through his fingers.

Dinner had been a mistake.

He'd wrongly thought that he and Nora would catch up, talk a bit about the past, that it would be an innocent opportunity to reminisce about an easier time. Before his world had crashed around his feet. He'd craved that with blinding necessity.

Instead, he'd spent the ten minutes she'd been in his penthouse trying desperately to keep his hands occupied so he didn't pull her into his arms to see if she tasted as good as she smelled. To see exactly what was under that black dress that showcased a body he hadn't remembered being so difficult to ignore.

You didn't seduce an old friend the moment she crossed your threshold. It was uncivilized and smacked of the kind of thing a man with his reputation would do. He'd done his share of perpetuating the myths surrounding his wickedness, mostly because it amused him.

Nora deserved better.

The problem was he had no interest in eating. At all. He'd developed an intense fixation with the hollow between Nora's breasts, which were scarcely contained by the bits of fabric that composed her dress.

You didn't stare at an old friend's rack, no matter how clearly she was inviting you to.

There were probably some other rules he should be reciting to himself right about now, but hell if he could remember what they were.

It had been too long since he'd had a woman in his bed; that was the problem. Nora Winchester O'Malley shouldn't be the one inciting him to break that fast. If he wanted to make the evening about catching up with an old friend, that was in his power to do.

"You're right," he allowed with a nod. "I didn't answer the question. I invited you to dinner because I wanted to thank you for being a good friend to me. The scales were unbalanced."

"Oh." Disappointment shadowed her gaze but she blinked and it was gone. "So dinner was motivated by the need to say thank you. For both of us, it seems."

"It seems."

That should have dispelled the sensual, tight awareness between them. That had been his intent. But she smiled and it lit up her face, inviting him in, warming up the places inside that had been cold since the plane crash that had changed everything.

"I feel properly thanked. Do you?" she asked.

"For what?" he nearly growled as he fought to stop himself from yanking her into his arms.

"For the food, silly." Her hands fisted on her hips. "That's the whole reason I asked you to dinner, remember?"

Yes, he did. They were two old friends. Nothing

more. He had to remember that her labeling it a date might not mean the same thing to her as it did to him.

"Everyone has been properly thanked." He drained his wineglass and scouted for the bottle. The bite of the aged red centered him again. "Are you ready to eat?"

"Depends on what you've got on the menu."

His gaze collided with hers and yes, she'd meant that exactly the way it sounded. Her smile slipped away as they stared at each other, evaluating, measuring, seeking. Perhaps he'd been going about this evening all wrong and the best course of action was to let their sizzling attraction explode.

But he couldn't help but think that if that happened, he'd miss out on the very thing he'd craved—friendship.

Four

Somehow, Reid dialed back his crushing desire and escorted Nora into the dining room. Maybe eating would take the edge off well enough to figure out what he wanted from this evening. And how to get it.

Since the servants had the night off, he played the proper host and served the gazpacho his chef had prepared earlier that day.

"This looks amazing, Reid," Nora commented and dug in.

A woman with a healthy appetite. Reid watched her eat out of the corner of his eye, which wasn't hard since she was sitting kitty-corner to him at the long teakwood table that he'd picked up on a trip to Bangalore.

The hard part was reminding his body that they'd

moved on to dinner. It didn't seem to have gotten the message. Friendship or seduction? He had to pick a direction. Soon.

"I trust it's sufficient?" he asked without a trace of irony as Nora spooned the last bite into her candy-pink mouth. Not only had she actually eaten, she'd done it without mussing her lipstick.

That was talent. Of course, now his gaze couldn't seem to unfasten from her mouth as she nodded enthusiastically.

"So great. I'm jealous of your private chef." She sighed dramatically. "I wish I had one. I have to cook for myself, which I don't mind. But some days, it sure would be nice to pass that off to someone else."

"Why don't you hire someone?" he suggested. "It's truly worth it in the end to have control over the fat and sodium content of what goes into your body."

"When did you become a health nut?"

"When I realized I wasn't going to live forever and that every bad thing I put in my mouth would speed me on my way to the grave."

It was a throwaway comment that any man in his thirties might make, but he actually meant it. When you spent a lot of time alone, you needed a hobby. His was his health. He read as many articles and opinion pieces about longevity as he could, tailoring his workouts and eating habits around tried-and-true practices. At one point, he'd even hired a personal dietician but fired him soon after Reid had realized he knew more than the "professional."

Staying healthy was a small tribute to his late mother and sister. They'd had their lives cut short, so Reid had decided he'd live as long as he could. And he wanted to be in the best shape possible for that.

"Good point. I wish it was as simple as you make it sound." She smiled wistfully. "But my bank account doesn't allow for things like private chefs."

He did a double take. "Did something happen to your father's fortune?"

Surely not. The scandal of Carson Newport's parentage wouldn't have reached the epic proportions that it had if Sutton were broke. Word was that Newport wanted as much of Winchester's estate as he could get his hands on. Though they'd crossed paths a few times, Newport wasn't someone Reid spoke to about private matters, so he could only speculate. But he didn't think Newport was in it for the money. Vengeance, more likely. Which was a shame. Winchester had it coming, but that meant Nora would be caught up in the drama, as well.

Perhaps Newport had already gotten his mitts on Nora's share?

But she shook her head. "Oh, no. Dad's money is well intact. I just don't have any of it. Walking away from Chicago meant walking away from everything. Including my trust fund."

Reid blinked. "Really? You renounced your inheritance?"

"Really. I don't want a dime of that money. It's tainted with the blood of all the people my dad has hurt over the years anyway. Plus, money is the root of all evil, right?" She shrugged one shoulder philosophically. "I've been much happier without it."

"*Love* of money is the root of all evil," Reid automatically corrected. Nearly everyone got that quote wrong. "It's a warning against allowing money to control you. Allowing it to make you into a terrible person in order to get more."

"Is that a dig at my dad?"

It had actually been a dig at his own father, not hers. Reid contemplated her before responding truthfully. "No. But it applies."

Sutton Winchester was cut from the same cloth as John Chamberlain, no doubt. Nora's father just hadn't had the courtesy to rid the world of his evil presence the way Reid's father had. Not yet anyway.

"Oh, have you dealt with my dad, then?"

Her slight smile said she knew exactly how much of a bastard her father was, but that didn't mean she deserved the full brunt of Reid's honest opinion of the man. Whether this evening consisted of two friends reconnecting or two friends connecting in a whole new way remained to be seen, but he imagined bad-mouthing Nora's father wouldn't benefit either scenario.

"Let's just say that we've got a solid truce and as long as he stays in his corner, I stay in mine."

That was a mild and very politically correct way to put it. Because when it came to business, Winchester fought dirty. His misdeeds had included paying off a judge to rule against a Chamberlain Group rezoning request, planting a spy at a relatively high level in Reid's organization and—the pièce de résistance—attempting to poison Chamberlain Group's reputation in the media with false allegations about Reid's ties to the mob. Winchester had gall. Reid had patience, influence and money—he'd won in the end.

"Well, I'm sure my father is the poster child for what happens to people who love money more than their own family," she said without hesitation. "It's part of the reason I left. I got tired of living the life of a socialite, doing nothing more meaningful than being photographed in the latest fashion or showing up at a charity event. Money doesn't buy anything worthwhile."

He topped off both wineglasses and served the main course, cold lamb and pasta, then picked up the thread of the conversation. "When used correctly, money is a tool that makes life better."

"Doesn't seem to have done that for you," she pointed out, tilting her wineglass toward him in emphasis. "You shut yourself up in this billion-dollar prison. I've been in your presence twice now, and I have yet to see any evidence that money has made you happy."

What would she say if he agreed with her? If he

said that money had done nothing but give his father the power to rip away Reid's soul? First by never being any kind of a father figure and then by taking his family with him on his journey to judgment day. The elder Chamberlain had picked his three-million-dollar Eclipse 550 as his weapon of choice, crashing the small jet deliberately and killing his wife and daughter.

Reid hadn't been on board. He'd been too busy chasing that next dollar.

Scary how alike he and his father were. You could run, but you couldn't hide from genetics. That's why Reid hadn't hesitated to say no when Nash came looking for someone to take in Sophia's twins. Reid wasn't father material. Reid was barely human material.

Money hadn't insulated him from heartache; it only afforded him the means to create what Nora called a prison. To him, it was a refuge.

"I like being alone," he finally said. "Having more money than the Bank of Switzerland allows me the luxury of kicking people out of my presence whenever I deem it necessary."

"Is that a warning?" Her smile bloomed instantly, zapping him in the gut. "Play nice or you'll see the backside of the door lickety-split?"

No, that wasn't what was on his mind, especially not when she treated him to the full force of her smile. Because now he was wondering what that mouth would feel like under his. She had to be a hell of a kisser— among other things.

"It's a fact," he said hoarsely as his throat went dry. "Take it as you will. Though in all fairness, few people ever cross the threshold in the first place, so all bets are off as to how quickly I might show you the way out."

"Hmm." Her gaze warmed as she perused him with an undisguised once-over, which raised the tension a painful notch. "So you're saying this is a bit of a unique experience?"

"Extremely."

She wasn't eating now. Neither was he. He was busy trying to keep his hands in his lap; even reaching for a fork might end up becoming a reason to abandon dinner entirely for a shot at experiencing Nora's kiss for himself.

"I've heard quite the opposite." She leaned an elbow on the table, drawing closer to him and wafting the scent of vanilla and strawberries in his direction.

That nearly pushed him over the edge. Other women smelled like thinly veiled invitations to carnal pleasures. Nora smelled like something he hadn't experienced in a very long time—innocence. He wanted her in a way he hadn't wanted anything he could recall in his life.

"Really?" he murmured. "What have you heard?"

Lies, exaggerations and wishful thinking, if it was any of the crap he knew was being passed around regarding his sex life. If she'd come here expecting an introduction to the forbidden side of pleasure, she'd leave disappointed.

"Nothing that I believed."

Her guileless blue eyes found his, warming him in a totally different way from anything she'd done thus far. "Really?"

She shrugged. "I know you. Those who are spreading rumors don't."

And perhaps that was true. They'd been friends, confidants and sometimes partners in crime. She seemed to still get him in a way no one else ever had. It thickened their connection and he liked that there was more here than just physical attraction. Liked how her innocence and strength of spirit promised to heighten their unique experiences.

All at once, he found himself in the middle of a paradox. The question here wasn't whether this evening would end in friendship or seduction, but how in the hell he'd gotten to a place where he wanted both.

Nora couldn't get over the jumpy, fluttery sensation in her stomach that Reid's intense stare produced.

Otherwise, she'd eat the exceptional lamb and pasta he'd placed in front of her instead of indulging in a third glass of wine that was probably going to get her into trouble before too long.

Because all she could think about was kissing Reid until he smiled.

He had hidden depths that he wasn't sharing with her. She could sense there was so much more behind his enigmatic brown eyes, so much pain she hoped to banish. She wanted to make him happy again. Was it so bad to be imagining that she could?

As he picked up his wineglass, she noted he hadn't eaten much, either. Too caught up in the conversation or just not hungry? Swirling the red wine, he watched it settle and then glanced at her, his gaze hot and full of something she wanted to explore. But she didn't know how to get to the next level.

"You might well be the only person in the world qualified to say you know me," he finally said, his voice huskier than normal, as if he had a catch in his throat the wine couldn't quite wash down.

She tried to laugh it off but the shock of his words wouldn't let her. "I was expecting you to argue with me. You know, say something along the lines of 'that was a long time ago.'"

"It was," he acknowledged with a tip of his head. "But not so long ago that I've forgotten how much I enjoyed our friendship. We never pulled punches with each other. I could always be honest with you about everything. We had something real that I foolishly let slip away."

Wow. That nearly knocked her flat. She'd moved on, but that didn't mean she hadn't mourned the loss of their friendship.

"It was a long time ago," she repeated inanely. "We can let bygones be bygones."

"You give me a lot of grace." He stood and held out

his hand. "Since I'd like to continue the tradition of being honest, I've lost interest in eating. Come with me."

Nora's pulse rate shot into the stratosphere. Was this the part where he planned to take her up on the invitation of her dress? The part where she got to find out what came after dinner?

Only one way to find out. She reached out and clasped his hand, allowing him to draw her to her feet. Awareness bled through her, tightening her breasts and heating her from the inside out. Her knees shook a bit, causing her stilettos to wobble in the deep pile of the runner that led from the dining room to the living room, where the breathtaking view of the Chicago skyline was eclipsed only by the sheer beauty of the man lightly caressing her knuckle with his thumb.

He stopped near the window and dropped her hand in favor of placing his palms on her shoulders. Then he positioned her directly in front of him so she faced the city. Their reflections blurred the neon lines of the buildings. She watched as he bent his head toward her neck.

"I like the picture you make," he murmured in her ear. "You and the vibrant city together."

His breath fanned across her sensitized skin, raising goose bumps and heat in an impossible mix of responses. But she couldn't have controlled her reaction if she'd tried. Okay, part of the excitement came from feeling safe, from feeling that she could trust Reid. But it also came from having those handy images from earlier pop back into her head. The X-rated ones.

His heat burned her back but she must have forgotten all the warnings she'd ever heard about staying away from fire because all she wanted to do was press backward into it. Let the power of attraction and desire sweep her away into an experience she suddenly wanted more than her next breath.

"I like you in that picture, too," she informed him. "In the spirit of being honest, I'm thinking about what that picture might look like if you kissed me."

The subtlest shift of his body toward hers was the only outward sign he gave that he'd heard what she said. Then she felt his fingers in her hair, lifting it away from her back, to be replaced with his lips at the hollow of her shoulder.

The shock of his kiss buckled her knees and she threw her hands up to steady herself against the window with a moan she couldn't bite back. She watched his reflection in the glass as he worked his way up the column of her throat, nibbling at her skin. She let her head list to the side to give him better access, but couldn't stop watching their reflections.

It was stimulating. Unreal. Unique.

He flattened his palms against her arms, sliding them upward until they covered her hands, pinning them against the glass. His torso aligned with her back and his hips nestled against her backside, nudging his thick erection into place at the small of her back.

Oh, my. That hard length spoke of his intent. If she wasn't ready for this, now would be the time to say so.

Her mouth opened. And then closed.

Didn't she deserve a night of passion with a man who made her feel alive for the first time in a long time? There was no shame in two people coming together like this, as long as everyone understood it was a fling, and nothing more. Her heart was permanently closed, but that didn't mean her body was, too.

Or was she trying to talk herself into something because she'd decided it was time to move on and had chosen Reid as the barometer of her success or failure? After all, who'd established that this was a fling? No one. They'd just had a conversation about their connection, their prior friendship and Reid's admission that he'd let her slip away, only to regret it.

"Reid," she breathed and he answered the plea with a firm full-body press that she felt all the way to her core.

One of his hands raced down her arm, tangled in her hair to cup the back of her head, turning it. And then his lips found hers. The kiss overwhelmed her, sucking her down a rabbit hole of pleasure even as her fingers curled against the glass, scrabbling for purchase against the slick surface.

There was none to be had. Reid took her deeper still, so she was even more off balance. He slowly drew her head backward as he added his tongue to the mix, licking in and out of her mouth in a sensuous rhythm that she responded to instantly, meeting him in the middle in a clash.

Obviously he didn't want to talk.

The kiss raged on as they tasted each other. The glass under her palms kept her upright, but barely, as Reid shoved a knee between her legs, his thigh rubbing near the place that needed his touch the most. The angle wasn't good enough. She arched her back, thrusting her hips backward, seeking relief for that sweet ache.

Cool air swept along her backside and she realized he'd hiked her dress up to her waist. His palm smoothed down the globe of her rear and she found enough of her brain was still functioning to be thankful Eve had talked her into a thong. The heat of his hand against her bare skin made her quake. Coupled with the friction of his thigh, she nearly came apart then.

"So responsive," he murmured, his lips moving against her collarbone as his hands explored her uncovered lower half. Helpless, she let him as sensations knifed through her.

His hand slid around to caress her abdomen and then lower and lower still, toying with the waistband of her panties until his fingers disappeared inside to cup her intimately.

She gasped as one finger slid between her folds, exactly where the flame burned the hottest.

This was all upside down and backward—literally. When making love to a woman, you started at the top and worked your way down. And you faced each other.

Reid had completely redefined seduction. She couldn't stop herself from reacting heavily to it, especially as she watched herself being pleasured in the reflection from the window. This must be what they meant when they whispered of his unusual tastes. She was an instant slave to it.

As he relentlessly drove her higher, she spiraled her hips against his hand and moaned his name. Her lids drifted shut for a brief moment until he drew off one shoulder of her dress, peeling it away from her breast. Her nipple hardened as it popped into view and he pushed her forward until it touched the glass. The shock of the cold surface against her heated flesh, coupled with his hand between her legs... It was too much.

She crested and cried out as the powerful orgasm overtook her. She would have collapsed if he hadn't snaked a hand around her waist, holding her tight against him, giving her a ringside seat to watch her half-naked reflection as she came, his fingers still deep inside her.

It was the single most erotic encounter of her admittedly tame life and she wanted more, with a fierceness she didn't recognize.

"That was amazing," he murmured in her ear as she settled. He withdrew and finally turned her in his arms to back her up against the window again.

"I think that's supposed to be my line." Breathlessly, she blinked up at him, suddenly shy now that they were facing each other. She'd just had the orgasm of her life, almost fully clothed, and he barely seemed ruffled. What had started as a ploy to get a smile out of him had swiftly become something else, something she'd been helpless to stop.

Now she wanted to return the favor. Without waiting for his okay, she curved her fingers around his jaw and pulled him down into a scorching kiss.

He met her and then some, the kiss spiraling into the stratosphere as they picked up where they'd left off a moment ago. She let her hands wander down his chest and found his waistband, then yanked his shirt from his pants so she could burrow underneath. The smooth skin of his back felt like heaven under her palms and she touched him to her heart's content.

Reid groaned into her mouth, even as he deepened the kiss, changing the angle, tongue hot and hard against hers.

Beep. The sound registered…somehow…and she pulled back from his drugging kiss. "Was that my phone?"

Reid blinked. "Mine is on silent."

Of course it was. He'd clearly set aside this evening to focus on her, but she wasn't in the position where she could do the same. Declan could be hurt or sick. Dismayed, she stared at Reid as reality came rushing back. "I'm sorry. I have to check that."

She stepped out of his arms, nearly weeping with need, not the least of which was a desire to make him feel as good as he'd done for her.

Scouting around for her clutch—which she hadn't seen in who knew how long—she finally found it at the wet bar, leaning up against the granite backsplash. She fished her phone from the depths and her heart plunged into her stomach as she saw Grace's name on the screen.

Nora had been letting her carnal side come out to play while something bad had happened to her son. A single mom shouldn't be dating, not while her kid was still so young. It was unforgivable. But then she read the text message and breathed a sigh of relief.

"Sorry," she called over her shoulder. "Declan is staying in an unfamiliar place and my sister just wanted me to know that he went down for the night without any fuss."

Thank God. Her pulse still thundered in her throat as she tapped back a quick message to Grace, noting it was nearly ten o'clock, the hour she'd said she'd be home. Grace had probably thought her timing was impeccable, that Nora was no doubt already in the car on her way back.

Good thing they'd been interrupted. This craziness with Reid—it wasn't her. She had responsibilities that she'd forgotten instantly the moment he'd touched her.

She slipped her phone back into her clutch and stood. When she faced Reid again, something had shifted in the atmosphere.

"Who's Declan?" he asked smoothly, his expression frozen into a mask she didn't recognize.

The hot, exciting man of a few moments ago had vanished. The one in its place had a hard, merciless outer shell that warned her to back off.

"Declan is my son. He's two."

Reid's expression didn't waver as a shadow fell over it. "You failed to mention that you were a mother. Deliberately?"

"What, like I was trying to hide it?" She laughed self-consciously. Hadn't she mentioned Declan? He was the light of her life. But then she and Reid hadn't really talked, not the way two old friends did who were catching up on each other's lives. "It never came up. I was married for almost five years before Sean died. We had a son together. It's relatively normal."

"Dinner was a mistake." Reid swiftly crossed to her and put an impersonal hand under her elbow, guiding her toward the door. His touch nearly made her weep— because it was so different from the way he'd touched her moments ago.

Stung, she pulled her arm free. "What's wrong with you, Reid? I'm suddenly no longer attractive because I have a kid?"

"Yes."

He offered no further explanation as Nora stared at him, her mouth hanging open. "That's a pretty ridiculous statement. Lots of women who are very attractive have children."

"I'm not dating any of them," he countered. "Nor am I dating you. Kids are a deal-breaker."

"I didn't know we had a deal." She crossed her arms over her midsection, very much fearing she was about to throw up. "I thought we were reconnecting while I was in town. I never expected this to go any further than one or two nights, tops. What does my son have to do with that?"

Everything, apparently, but Reid had said his piece. His mouth was a firm, grim line as he extended his hand, indicating the door she was supposed to be disappearing through. The connection she'd felt, the attraction and good memories of the past, all of it fled instantly. Nora suddenly felt both cheap and ripped off at the same time.

Her Achilles' heel—vulnerability—nearly overwhelmed her. But she didn't have to take what he was dishing out. She was in charge of her destiny. This shadowy, unfathomable stranger wasn't the man she'd known once upon a time.

"Nice. I guess your reputation *is* quite overblown." She whirled and marched toward the door before he caught glimpse of the hurt that was surely spreading over her face. "Don't worry. I won't tell anyone you're too obnoxious to sleep with," she called over her shoulder, slamming the door behind her.

Five

All of Reid's employees gave him a wide berth for two days.

Which was relatively normal, but usually it was out of respect for his preference to be alone. Lately, it was to avoid his wrath as he found fault with everyone in his path.

For the fourth time since his morning coffee, Reid was confronted with yet another example of ineptitude as he exited the elevator on the forty-seventh floor. The meeting he'd just attended across town had been full of pompous blowhards who wouldn't know compromise if it bit them in their butts. Traffic had been impossible and now this—the sign in the vestibule, the one that was supposed to greet visitors, had fallen over. And not even the right way. The front lay facedown on the short pile carpet, its blank backside displaying a whole lot of nothing in the direction of the ceiling.

He stormed through the door into the reception area of Metropol's administrative office. "Mrs. Grant."

His admin glanced up from her computer. "Mr. Chamberlain."

He rolled his eyes. Mrs. Grant was the only person he'd ever allow to speak to him with that kind of snarkiness and that was only because she was irreplaceable. "Call building maintenance. The welcome sign has fallen over. And while you're on the phone with them, ask them whether they like their paychecks. It's inexcusable to have a hotel with this shoddy of an appearance. Guests can stay in a lot of hotels that aren't mine. We want them… What are you looking at?"

Mrs. Grant stared at him as if he'd grown another head. "Are you finished?"

"Just getting started," he shot back.

She tsked. "Not with maintenance, you're not. Unless you'd like to run this hotel all by yourself?"

"What are you talking about? The Metropol has a maintenance crew that employs a hundred people—"

"And those numbers will dwindle down to one surly CEO if you keep it up," she interrupted mildly. "We've already had two resignations today alone. I'm not calling maintenance, so you can forget all that bluster and nonsense. Watch and learn."

Mrs. Grant stood and skirted him, jerking her head

toward the vestibule. Was everyone determined to extract their pound of his flesh? After that disappointing meeting that had been a colossal waste of his time, all he wanted to do was go to his office, where he could decompress by himself.

She pushed open the frosted glass door and held it open, refusing to budge until he followed her. With a long-suffering sigh, he did.

Pointedly, she widened her eyes as she bent over and righted the sign. "See? No maintenance crew required, Mr. Chamberlain. No small children were harmed in the fixing of this problem."

Small children. It wasn't a dig, as Mrs. Grant had no idea what had transpired between Reid and Nora two days ago. But it felt like a strong reproach of his behavior all the same.

He didn't like it. He'd been doing his level best to forget about Nora Winchester—or Nora O'Malley, or whatever she called herself these days—and the reminders were not welcome.

"You're right," he acknowledged gruffly. "I could have resolved that one myself, but the rest of the issues—"

"Are a normal part of doing business." She crossed her arms over her nondescript suit and eyed him. "What's wrong with you lately? Something's bothering you."

How did she know that? Suspicious, he eyed her back. "I have no idea what you're referring to."

"Save it, dear. You and I both know that you're a

pussycat under that grumpy exterior. Someone got you all worked up and you're going to have to fix it before too long. Even you can't do it all yourself."

Want to bet?

He almost said it out loud. But that wouldn't make Mrs. Grant any less right.

He deflated under the sympathetic gaze of his admin. "Sorry. I've been a bit beastly, I admit."

"Why don't you take the rest of the day off?" she suggested. "It's nearly five anyway. I know you like to work monstrously long hours, but I promise your empire will not collapse if you leave the helm a couple of hours early."

Working long hours prevented his mind from wandering. That's when the grief crept up on him, whacking him the hardest—when he wasn't prepared.

He nodded, but only because the idea of getting out from under Mrs. Grant's all-too-shrewd gaze had a lot of appeal. "Have a good night, then."

She would handle his email and take calls on his behalf. Such was the benefit of having an admin who was so well trained; he could disappear for a few hours and she'd steer the ship in the right direction.

But when he walked in through the door of his penthouse, he caught the faintest scent of vanilla and strawberries, and the memory of Nora in his arms, as she'd looked while reflected in the window, exploded in his mind. The image of her—hot, unrestrained, pleasured—

appeared as if by magic in the glass, multiplying exponentially across all the panes until she surrounded him.

Yeah, he couldn't blame his bad mood on anything except the disappointment of really connecting with Nora the other night only to find out the truth about her: she had a kid. It was fine. He preferred being alone anyway. A woman would only complicate his life to the nth degree and he didn't need that.

Grimly, he turned his back on the floor-to-ceiling windows and sought out a bottle of fifty-year-old Dalmore. The scotch burned down his throat but even the heavy scent of toffee and alcohol couldn't overpower the memories of the woman he'd nearly bedded two nights ago.

Nearly bedded, but hadn't, thanks to the fortuitous interruption that had revealed Nora's lies.

Oh, she'd had no problem mentioning she'd been married. A widow, he could deal with. A mom, he could not. And she hadn't bothered to inform him that she had a kid in tow. He couldn't handle kids, couldn't handle the guilt of not having the ability to care for one. If he'd wanted to find out how crappy of a father he'd be, he'd have taken Sophia's twins when offered the chance, thank you very much.

The scotch had done the opposite of what he'd hoped. Instead of dulling his thoughts, it sharpened them as they drifted to Phoebe and Jude. His niece and nephew were fraternal twins, but they looked a lot alike. Because they resembled Sophia.

His mood fell off a cliff.

Sick of his own company, and tired of battling the pile of remorse on his shoulders, which weighed more every day, he yanked his phone out and called Nash. His brother answered on the first ring.

"Reid. Is everything okay?"

Worry tinged Nash's voice, thickening the ever-present guilt swirling around in Reid's gut along with the scotch. Guilt that he hadn't saved his sister and mother. Guilt because Nash had stepped up where Reid had failed. Guilt over how hurt Nora had looked after Reid had unceremoniously shoved her out the door. And then he still had some guilt left over for how he'd treated his staff these past few days.

"Yeah. Does something have to be wrong for me to call?"

Nash didn't hesitate. "Uh, usually. But if this is just a random drive-by call, that's okay. How are you?"

Lonely.

Reid cursed to himself. Where the hell had that come from? Nora was not right about that. He liked being alone. Except he'd enjoyed her company. She'd made the darkness inside…bearable. More than bearable. She'd eased it. Especially when she'd kissed him, when she'd opened up, inviting him into her warmth. Disappointment about Nora's pint-sized complication didn't begin to describe it.

"I'm fine," Reid lied. "How are the twins?"

"They're three. It's an extension of the terrible twos,

which apparently lasts until they're eighteen." Nash's chuckle rumbled across the line. "Gina has been threatening to put them in military school, but of course they've latched onto the idea like it's some big game. 'Will we learn how to shoot guns?' they asked. Both of them."

"Phoebe, too?" Reid fell onto the sofa that faced the view of the Sears Tower, propping the phone up against his shoulder so he could retrieve his drink from the coffee table. "That seems odd for a girl."

Nash's shrug was nearly audible over the line. "Last week, she wanted to be a ninja. Lest you forget, Sophia never cared about quote-unquote 'girl stuff.' Phoebe wants to do whatever Jude is doing. You should visit. See them for yourself."

He should. They were his blood, too, same as Sophia. But he couldn't. The twins were one more huge reminder of how he hadn't been able to be what those kids needed. How he couldn't be a father because he lacked...*something*. There was a big, gaping hole where the ability to nurture and care about other human beings should be, a hole formed by genetic predisposition and further hollowed out when the family he loved had been ripped away. No way would Reid ever care about someone again. Not to that degree.

He couldn't risk it. Not with Sophia's kids, not with Nora's. Not even with Nora herself.

"Chamberlain Group is in a transition stage, so it would be difficult to get away," he explained even as his gut churned over the fabrication. Chamberlain Group always came first, regardless of what was happening internally at his company. It was safer that way. He controlled what happened and that would never change.

"Yeah, that's what you always say." Nash spoke to someone else in the room, his voice muffled as if he'd covered the speaker with his hand. Then, more clearly, he said, "Gina says hi and wants to know if you're seeing anyone."

"What? Why would she ask that?" Reid scrambled for an explanation as to how his brother's wife would have heard about Reid's date with Nora. Had Nora told a bunch of people? Surely she wouldn't be so indiscreet. "I'm not seeing anyone and the media likes to exaggerate stories of my love life anyway. Has Gina heard something? Tell me who's talking about my—"

"Relax. She didn't hear anything in the media. I would have told you so, as I know how much you value your privacy. Gina has a friend she thought you might like and wanted to introduce you since you're not seeing someone. That's all."

Reid's conscience kicked in as he envisioned having dinner with this new woman the way he'd had dinner with Nora. A different woman would sit in that chair kitty-corner to his at the big table. A different woman would drink from his wineglass, peering up at him over the rim.

No. Those memories belonged to Nora. He never brought women home in the first place and now Nora was stamped all over his penthouse. Irrevocably. This was why being alone was better.

"That's nice. Tell her thank you, but no. I'm pretty busy right now."

"So you *are* seeing someone." Nash laughed. "I thought your protests a minute ago were a little too vehement for a simple question. Who is she?"

"I'm not." Reid sighed. Who was he kidding? He'd been in such a bad mood because he didn't like how things had ended. Because he'd secretly wished for a different outcome and couldn't see a way around the cold, hard facts. "But only because it turned out she has a kid."

"Still sticking to that stupid rule I see. You have no idea what you're missing out on. Kids are great and if you like this woman, you should spend more time with her and her child before drawing such a hard line. What's the worst that could happen? You find out you can't stand children and you tell her it's not working out. But at least you tried."

"It's not that simple."

But it could have been. If he hadn't been so brutally final about motherhood being a deal breaker. If he hadn't freaked out as he had. Things had gotten intense and maybe he'd been looking for a way to break it up before something happened that he couldn't take back.

No kids was his rule. But he'd wielded it like a blunt instrument, desperate to reel back an encounter that had exploded into something much more than he'd expected it to be.

His guilty conscience roared to the forefront. If nothing else, he owed Nora an apology. The way he'd acted was inexcusable, especially given that neither of them was looking for anything permanent. Nora had even said one, two nights tops, and she didn't live in Chicago. He'd drawn a line that didn't matter in the long run because her kid wasn't a factor if they didn't even live in the same city.

"Why not?" Nash asked.

"I said some things that I probably shouldn't have. She probably wouldn't even take my call."

"So don't call her," Nash advised. "Go to her with as many flowers as you can carry, tell her you're sorry you're such a jackass and then make it up to her."

Reid bit back a self-deprecating laugh. "Really? That works?"

"Gina's nodding her head so hard, it's about to fly off."

His bad mood eased a little. "Thanks. I'll try it."

Nora made him feel alive. He wanted more of that, and if he handled the apology right, maybe he could have it. What was the worst thing that could happen?

Sutton Winchester was awake.

Nora liked it better when her father was asleep. Then she could pretend the reconciliation she'd secretly hoped for when she'd decided to come back to Chicago might actually happen. When he was coherent and could speak? Forget it.

After her father had demanded to meet Declan—a first for them both—she'd patiently waited for something akin to grandfatherly love to surface. And of course she'd gotten exactly what she should have expected: a comment about how her son looked nothing like a Winchester, which was somehow the fault of her marrying someone with strong Irish genes. Then came a scolding over the fact that she hadn't cashed the six-figure check Sutton had sent her so she could educate his grandson properly. Apparently private schools offered the only acceptable education for a Winchester. And so on.

Having her hopes dashed was exhausting. And after the debacle with Reid, Nora was sick of being disappointed. Since taking control of a bad situation had become her new mantra, she'd walked out of her father's hospital room without another word, taking Declan with her.

Medical personnel dressed in scrubs rushed by on both sides as she caught her breath in the hall. Not wanting to be in the way, Nora ducked into an alcove. From this vantage point, she glimpsed a similar alcove down the way and a familiar face popped into her field of vision.

Eve. And she wasn't alone. A man occupied the alcove with her. He had his back to Nora so she couldn't be certain of his identity, but his longish blond hair and authoritative stature gave her a big clue that it was either Brooks or Graham Newport, one of Carson's twin half brothers. Nora had met them all briefly yesterday for the first time and hadn't spent enough time with the brothers to tell them apart yet.

Her sister's expression made it clear they were having a heated conversation. Intrigued, Nora watched them for a few moments. She had zero prayer of hearing what they were saying since a good fifty yards and a sea of people separated them. But their body language told an interesting story: namely, that the two were far more comfortable with each other than Nora would have guessed. Their torsos and hips nearly met at least three times in the tight alcove and neither of them seemed inclined to shift away.

What in the world? Was Eve playing coy with one of the Newport twins to get dirt on Carson? Her sister had been furious over the inheritance grab Carson had initiated. Maybe she was trying to influence whichever brother she'd cornered into getting Carson to back off. That had to be it. The sparks between the two must be her imagination.

Declan tugged on Nora's skirt and held up his chubby arms, silently asking to be picked up in his little-boy language. She complied and hugged him close. This was all that mattered. The most important thing in her universe sat encased in her arms and she'd fight to shield Declan from the evils of the world as long as she could.

Men like her father would corrupt him, and men like Reid would hurt him.

So she'd keep doing this alone. Nothing had changed. Then why had dinner with Reid felt like the beginning of something different, only to have it all crash down around her?

"Sorry Grandpa turned out to be such a mean man," she murmured into his neck. "We'll figure out how to be the better person here. Somehow."

"Home," Declan told her.

"Yeah, soon," Nora promised, her heart aching at the thought of the empty house waiting for them both back in Silver Falls.

All she'd wanted from her night with Reid was companionship. A few moments of being treated like a woman again instead of a mom and widow. Over the years, he'd obviously become someone else, someone she didn't like, and she mourned the loss of her starry-eyed childhood vision of him the most.

When she stepped out of the alcove, Gracie appeared from around the corner.

"Oh, there you are," she called and halted. A harried nurse nearly plowed into her, so they both shuffled to the edge of the corridor. "I was looking for you to see if you wanted to watch a movie with me and Eve tonight. This bedside vigil is killing me. I could use a girls' night."

"Yes, absolutely." It sounded heavenly all at once, not to have to face a long evening alone. "Come to the guesthouse so I can put Declan to bed and we'll watch something there."

"Sure, that sounds great." Gracie glanced around the brightly lit hallway. "Have you seen Eve? I texted her but she hasn't responded."

"I'm here." Breathless, Eve skidded to a stop near Nora, the color in her cheeks high. "I was…um, on a conference call. What's up?"

Nora's brows lifted involuntarily at her sister's bald-faced lie, but she didn't call her on it. Instead, she tucked the information—both the cover-up and the fact that her sister had been cozying up with a member of the enemy camp—into her back pocket in case she needed it later. "Gracie and I were just organizing a movie night. You in?"

"Great, great." Eve nodded, but her gaze shifted over Nora's shoulder, obviously distracted by something. Or someone. "Eight o'clock?"

They all agreed on the time and Nora slipped away from the hospital with the excuse that Declan needed to take a nap. Which was true but Nora really needed to regroup after dealing with her father's domineering attitude.

Once she arrived at the guesthouse, Nora found herself too restless to lie down, though her body screamed with fatigue. She thought about how she should find a job when she got home. It had been nearly two years since Sean died and her dream of being a stay-at-home mom to a brood of children had died along with her husband. Before she'd married Sean, she'd dabbled in web design, but hadn't built up a freelance business worth hanging on to. Gracie was the Winchester sister with all the natural design skill, which she put to use in the fashion industry. Nora had just enough to get by. So maybe something else would present itself.

The day dragged and Nora was looking forward to movie night more than she'd have anticipated. She and her sisters had always been close before she'd left for Colorado, but they'd drifted apart as their circle of friends changed and the distance made it too difficult to spend quality time together. It was nice to pick up the threads of their relationship as if no time at all had passed.

Dinner was a somber affair for two and Declan picked at his food more so than usual.

"Eat your carrots," Nora said and nodded at the fruit snack pack she'd placed out of reach but within his line of sight as incentive. "Dessert is only for boys who finish their dinner."

"No. Now." Declan's stubborn little lip came out, signifying his Irish temper had started a slow simmer, threatening to boil over if he didn't get his way.

"Carrots. Then fruit snacks."

Nora forked her own microwavable mush into her mouth. The box might have been labeled Asian Noodles with Chicken but it sure didn't taste like much. Reid's nonchalant mention of a private chef drifted into her head. *As if.* That was just one more reason why it was better for them to have parted ways. The man had too much money and it had shaded his view of mere mortals. Not everyone got to hire staff to cater to their every whim.

If Nora had wanted to be a slave to the all-mighty dollar, she'd have taken Sutton Winchester's dirty money and lived high on the hog without a thought of the stipend the military sent her every month. To do so felt like a betrayal of Sean's sacrifice for his country. That money was hers, sent from beyond the grave by the man she'd loved.

Even though Declan exhibited more drama than a group of high school cheerleaders at prom, the carrots ultimately disappeared into her baby's mouth. Fruit snacks finally in hand, Declan calmed down. Later, he even took a bath without objection, then went straight down in his crib, leaving Nora tired but victorious.

Movie night could officially begin.

Except when she emerged from the back of the guesthouse where the bedrooms lay, she saw her phone was flashing. She had a message. It was from Eve. Have to cancel tonight.

What in the world? She texted her sister back: Hot date?

The return message came back so fast, Nora wondered if her sister had been sitting on her phone: No, of course not! Why would you think that? That's ridiculous. Gracie and I decided to stay at the hospital with Dad.

At the hospital…where whichever Newport twin

she'd been having such a heated conversation with had last been spotted. Nora sent a follow-up message: Seems like the scenery there is pretty good. Sure you don't have extra motivation to stick around? Maybe in the form of a MAN?

No.

Well. That was a clipped response if she'd ever heard one, and Eve's caginess only increased Nora's curiosity. But she let it slide, too disappointed in the lost movie night to worry about it for the time being.

But why Gracie had also canceled—that remained a mystery. One Nora would like to solve. Experience told her she had a long night ahead of her, heavy with reflection and loneliness. This was when she missed having a significant other the most. She should be used to it by now, especially since she'd pretty much decided that she'd be single the rest of her life. How could she possibly ever let herself fall in love again? She couldn't. So she'd be alone by default.

Mostly, she was okay with it. But not on a night when she'd expected to have company.

Nora tapped up Grace's contact info, intending to send her a message to ask what was up, when the speaker near the front door beeped. George, her father's gatekeeper, called out, stating she had a visitor.

Relieved, Nora couldn't press the intercom button fast enough. "Yes, I'm expecting someone."

Gracie wasn't canceling after all. Eve must have been

using Grace as a cover and forgotten to actually get their stories straight before their youngest sister bailed on her. Too bad. Maybe Grace had the dirt on Eve's shenanigans.

Whatever the case, Nora was happy she wasn't going to spend the evening alone. Again.

Nora swung the door open, smile in place. But it instantly slipped.

Reid Chamberlain stood on her doorstep, holding a red tricycle in one hand and what had to be five dozen of the most amazingly full and beautiful flowers she'd ever seen.

Nora blinked but the image didn't change. "What are you doing here?"

"Apologizing."

Their gazes met and he pulled her into the moment, just as he'd done the first time in his office. And the second time at his door. *Mesmerizing*. That was the only word she could come up with for his mahogany-brown eyes. A sharp, quick memory of the last time she'd seen him, of what his hands had done to her body, weakened her knees.

She straightened them, refusing to be affected. Reid was mercurial, talking about connections and friendship in one breath and then turning into an implacable wall the next. This man wanted nothing to do with her son and therefore, he wanted nothing to do with her. He was moody and morose and far too complex. She'd let him hurt Declan over her dead body.

Reid held out the tricycle. "This is for your son. If you'll accept it. No strings attached."

The fact that he'd offered that first, before the flowers, knocked away a chunk of Nora's ire, quite against her will. She took it from his outstretched hand, but she had to use both of hers. The tricycle was much heavier than it appeared and he'd been holding it one-handed. "Thank you. He'll love it and he needs activities to keep him occupied. This was a nice gesture."

"I don't make nice gestures," he reminded her. She realized that she had no idea what motivated him, what governed his thoughts, why he shifted moods like quicksilver.

She set the shiny red tricycle inside the house, just to the left of the door where it was out of the way.

"That's right." Crossing her arms over her chest to ease the ache caused by the sound of his smooth voice, she eyed him. "You must want something. What is it?"

Her body hadn't gotten the message that Reid Chamberlain wasn't on the menu, apparently.

"For you to forgive me. I behaved badly the other night. I'm sorry."

A hint of the smile she'd once craved played at his lips as he stood there waiting for her response.

"For which part? The orgasm or for kicking me out?"

The ghost smile vanished. "I would never apologize for pleasuring you. It was an experience I'll never forget. One of the best I've ever had."

Oh, my. His gaze sharpened on hers and heat arced

between them as she flooded with longing. "But we didn't even get to you. We were interrupted."

As if either of them needed the reminder.

"Make no mistake. It was just as good for me as it was for you. I'd do it again, anytime, anyplace."

She shuddered. She excited him and he'd enjoyed watching her as he touched her, aroused her, awakened her. It shouldn't be so stimulating. Not when they still had so much unsaid between them.

"I don't understand why you're here," she said faintly. "You said you didn't date women with kids."

"I'm making an exception if you'll let me."

His gaze bored into hers, communicating far more than his words did. He wanted her and was willing to break his rules. Only for her. She was ashamed that her soul latched onto the lovely thought so quickly.

She had to clarify what was and wasn't happening. Before things got out of hand. Again.

"Well, I'm not making any exceptions. Not when it comes to my son. I need to understand your intentions."

She needed to understand *Reid*.

He held out the flowers and waited until she took them. Merciful heaven, they were beautiful and smelled divine. She kind of wanted to throw them on the bed and roll around in them. Maybe with Reid—*after* he assured her he'd gotten over his aversion to moms. Declan was a part of her and Reid couldn't separate her from her son even if he tried. Nor would she let him.

"I intend to apologize," he repeated. "I can also explain why I don't date women with children. And why I'm standing on your doorstep, despite that. If more comes out of the evening, that's your choice."

Her heart tumbled a little at his sincerity. In a life where she mourned the loss of choices, being given one tipped the scales.

"Come in, then. But in the interest of full disclosure, my son is here. Asleep. But very much in the house and prone to waking up in need of a drink, crackers, his frog blanket, a missing stuffed animal and quite possibly a book that he'll have to have right that minute. Sometimes all of the above."

"I'll consider myself warned."

To his credit, Reid didn't hesitate to cross the threshold when she opened the door wider in invitation. He glanced around the lavishly appointed guesthouse with apparent appreciation for the priceless art on the walls and rare marble-inlaid floor. But he didn't comment and instead turned to face her in the foyer, which suddenly got a lot smaller despite the twenty-foot ceilings.

"Your son's name—it's Declan?" he asked out of the blue. "I want to refer to him appropriately."

"Yes." As an afterthought, she added, "O'Malley." But only because Reid had her all tripped up and sideways by making such a sweet effort.

"I remember. His father was killed in the line of duty."

Since the sudden lump in her throat wasn't conducive to talking, Nora nodded. She couldn't for the life of her recall telling him that.

"That's a legacy your boy should never forget." Reid pursed his lips. "I have some things I want to talk to you about. Do you mind if we sit down?"

"That sounds so somber." She tried to laugh it off but his expression didn't change. It almost made her wish they could slide back into the place they'd been a minute ago, when the atmosphere grew heavy with implication and attraction the longer they stared at each other. "Should I open a bottle of wine?"

He inclined his head. "Sure. A little liquid courage couldn't hurt."

"Feeling shy?" she teased, a little desperate to get things back on even ground as she crossed to the wine refrigerator behind the small bar in the great room. "Surely we're past that stage at this point."

"The wine is for you."

There came that ghost of a smile again and it did funny things to her insides. What would happen if he really let go? Did she want to find out? The last time they'd been in close proximity, she'd ended up hurt and confused. She didn't want to give Reid an opening to do that again. But after his apology and comments about Declan and his father, maybe she could trust him.

She popped the cork on the wine that she'd planned to share with Grace and Eve. At least she wasn't alone anymore. But whether that turned out to be a good thing or not remained to be seen.

Six

Reid accepted the wineglass from Nora's outstretched hand and downed a healthy sip. Despite what he'd told her, the wine was for him, too. The darkest period of his life wasn't an easy thing to spell out, but he owed her an explanation and he planned to give it to her.

Except he'd never talked to anyone about this stuff. Sure, lots of women had tried to dig into his moods and tendency to be a loner, usually with disastrous results— for them. He was more than happy to let them be disappointed. No one got to see inside him.

But for the first time, here he was about to spill his guts to a woman he'd hurt and then driven away. She should've been furious and full of righteous indignation, not settling in next to him on the leather sofa, her T-shirt stretching nicely over her gorgeous breasts.

When she'd arrived at his penthouse the other day in that little black dress, he'd had a hard time unsticking his tongue from the roof of his mouth. He'd have said that version of Nora was his favorite. He'd have been wrong.

Dressed for a night at home, Nora had a tantalizing, comfortable air about her that invited him to get cozy. He ached to take her up on that invitation. The woman vibrated with sensual, fresh energy 24/7, and he couldn't look away. Nor did he want to.

"Also in the interest of disclosure," Nora said before he could open his mouth, "I appreciate that you're leaving the direction of the evening up to me. I've become a bit of a control freak in the last little while and like to know that I'm driving the bus."

And instantly, that bit of information jump-started his libido again. He didn't mind a woman in control one iota and his imagination exploded with ideas designed to help her get there.

Starting with her on top of him—fully naked, because that was a bridge he'd yet to cross—head thrown back as she used her fingers to pleasure them both to her heart's content. Nora had painted her half-inch-long nails a whimsical purple and he couldn't stop imagining them wrapped around his erection. That picture wasn't going to work, at least not if he hoped to be honest with her instead of using sex as an excuse to avoid intimacy. Until now, that had been his usual go-to method.

"Noted." He cleared his throat. "I appreciate that the theme of the night is full disclosure. In that vein, I admit, I was upset about what I considered an omission on your part about your son."

Her brows came together as she processed that. "I didn't not tell you on purpose. It just never came up and honestly, it never occurred to me that it would be an issue. Lots of people in their thirties have kids. Personally, I'd find it more surprising to learn that a married couple didn't have kids. Wait." She reached out and placed a hand on his arm, her expression turning grave. "You *do* know how babies are made, right?"

A smile raced across his face before he could catch it and she lit up instantly. Which both aroused him and made him uncomfortable because he still didn't know if they were headed toward a reconciliation that might include sex.

He'd be happy if she accepted his apology and they acted like friends, just talking for a little while. Because he wanted that, too.

"You so rarely smile, Reid." Her hand didn't move from his arm and warmth bled through him as she talked. "I've missed it. That's one of your best features and I've always liked your smile. Do it more often."

"I would have sworn I'd permanently lost my smile." The fact that she'd dredged up something from his depths that he'd assumed was gone forever somehow made all of this easier. And harder. "I came to deliver flowers, a gift for Declan and an explanation. Smiles weren't included in the deal."

"Then I'll consider it a bonus." She sipped her wine, watching him over the rim. "What is the deal, then? You're going to give me your song and dance about how you like your freedom and a kid would only cramp your style and then what? We pick up where we left off in your penthouse?"

"Is that what you think this is about?"

She blinked but it was the only outward reaction she gave. "Of course. I'm a big girl. I can take it if kids are not your thing, as long as you're honest about it. I don't have stars in my eyes about some rosy future between us. We're hot for each other, and given the preview of what sex is going to be like between us, why dither around?"

"Because," he growled, "it's *not* like that. I'm not... There's nothing wrong with kids. It's me."

His throat tightened up so fast he couldn't breathe. A sip of wine didn't help.

"Hey."

She squeezed his arm and waited until he glanced at her before she continued.

"If it's not like that, I'm sorry." She peered up at him from under her lashes and the sincerity in her hazel eyes sucked him under. "Tell me what it's like, then. If you want to."

He wanted to. But how did you explain something

so deeply flawed about yourself to another person? Nora might be the kindest person on the planet, but she wouldn't easily accept what he had to tell her. And he couldn't stand the thought of that light in her eyes being snuffed when she found out just how messed up he truly was.

No. He actually *didn't* want to tell her. He'd operated out of pure selfishness for so long, he scarcely knew how to put someone else first. But Nora deserved to know the truth.

"You heard about Sophia?" he choked out. He might as well start at the beginning.

Nora's hand froze on his arm. "No."

"She died." Blunt. There was no other way to say it. Death was always blunt. And brutal. "About two years ago. My whole family was involved in a plane crash. I was the only one not on board."

"Oh, Reid." Her eyes filled with unshed tears. "I hadn't heard. I'm so sorry."

"Nash survived. Barely."

That hardly covered the emotional angst Nash had battled when he'd awoken in the hospital, in pain and facing months of recovery, only to realize he was the sole survivor. Guilt had burdened his brother for a while. But he'd eventually gotten over it. Reid never had.

"But no one else did?" Nora asked softly and her stricken expression said she already knew the answer.

"No. Everyone is gone. Sophia had two children who

weren't on board, either. Twins, a boy and a girl. Her ex-husband isn't in the picture, so her kids were essentially homeless."

Nora shook her head as the tears finally cascaded down her cheeks. "How awful for them. How old were they when it happened?"

"Babies."

His throat closed. Tiny, helpless babies, only a year old. And he'd ignored them in their most desperate hour. Never mind the turmoil he'd been thrown into while mourning the loss of his mother and sister—but not his father. The investigators at the scene had told him that the black box had recorded John Chamberlain confessing a multitude of sins and a desire to take his family to the grave with him.

Nora slid her hand down his arm, then threaded her fingers through his and clasped them tightly. He stared at their joined hands and something welled in his chest, squeezing it pleasantly. Providing wordless comfort that he didn't deserve.

He yanked his hand free before he came to rely too much on her warmth. He owed her the unvarnished truth and he wasn't close to done. "Nash and I fought about what to do. We were both single men with demanding careers. What did we know about raising kids? I... Well, we agreed we didn't want them to go to strangers, but the whole idea of becoming a father didn't sit well with me."

That was way too kind a way of putting it.

"Of course it didn't!" Nora's staunch support rang out in her tone. "You'd just lost your family, and grief is a terrible place to be in when trying to make decisions. I know. Trust me."

"No." Bleakly, he met her gaze and forced out the words that would destroy that fragile, brave sympathy in Nora's expression. "You don't know. You can't possibly understand. I abandoned them. I didn't want to be a father. I'm not loving and nurturing, nor do I have any desire to learn. My company is my life. I chose that over my sister's children and forced Nash's hand."

Nora's expression didn't change. It should have. She should have been scowling at him and blasting him with ugly words about what a horrible person he was. Because *that* would be the unvarnished truth.

Instead, she smiled as two more tears splashed down her cheeks. *Smiled*, and the smile held more understanding and grace than he could fully comprehend. Combined with her tears, it wrenched something open inside him and tears he almost couldn't contain pricked at his own eyelids.

Mortified, he blinked them back. Sorrow had no place here; he had no right to feel anything other than condemned. This was a recitation of his sins, plain and simple.

"What happened after that?" she murmured softly.

"Nash took them in," he admitted hoarsely. "He was the bigger man. I…couldn't. I'm selfish. I work eighty or ninety hours a week because my empire makes sense to me. That's why I wasn't on board the plane. I was in a meeting that I couldn't miss."

He should have been on that plane. Nash had insisted he'd tried to overpower their father with no success, but if both of them had been there, things might have turned out differently.

"Guilt is a killer," she said simply, and that nearly put him on his knees.

How had she zeroed in on that? She saw too much, understood too much. *She* was too much.

"Reid. Look at me," she commanded, and God help him, he did.

She took his wineglass and placed it next to hers on the low coffee table near the sofa. Slowly, she cupped his jaw in both of her hands and brought his lips to hers for a sweet, unending kiss that had nothing to do with sex. It was absolution.

And he didn't want it.

But he couldn't stop the freight train of his pulse as her goodness and light filled the cold places inside. Greedily, he soaked it up even as his own arms came up to encompass her, drawing her closer.

She broke off the kiss and touched his cheek with hers. "It's okay," she murmured. "I'm not going anywhere."

"You should," he said roughly even as he tightened his arms. "You should be kicking me out as unceremoniously as I did you the other night."

"Why? Because you made a decision you regret?" She tsked. "Who hasn't?"

It wasn't the same. But oh, dear God, he wanted it to be. Wanted to latch onto the simplicity of what she was trying to convey. That kind of liberty wasn't available to him. "You're making this out to be something it's not."

"Stop arguing with me!" She drew back and *now* she was scowling. "You listen to me. You are not a bad person because you didn't want to take in Sophia's children. Kids are a huge responsibility and more people should think about their capacity for parenthood before jumping into it. You want to know something? I think it's honorable that you don't let things go too far with a woman when she has a child."

Dumbfounded, he stared at her as his hands fell to the couch on either side of her. "What?"

"You heard me," she shot back fiercely. "A mom has more to think about than herself. You got that and immediately shut things down between us, even though I was all about the moment. It was nothing but fun and games to me. *You* were the bigger person in that scenario."

He shook his head but it didn't erase the spin she'd put on his actions. "That's—"

True. Yeah, he'd been selfishly thinking of himself the other night but in the end, he had found the force of will to step away, even though it had been the last thing he wanted to do. And that was the only honorable thing he'd done. "You're not listening to what I'm saying. I turned my back on my blood, on my sister. It's unforgivable."

She waved it off as if he'd admitted to taking the last cookie. "Are they being beaten at Nash's house? Starved?"

"No. He hired a great nanny and then fell in love with her. Gina is the best mom to those kids." Which was totally not the point. "I would have botched it."

"See?" She threw up her hands. "It all turned out like it should have. Some people call that fate. You, on the other hand, have moped around about it far too long."

"Moped?" Reid Chamberlain had a reputation for being dark and brooding. Reclusive and mysterious. He did not *mope*.

Her wide smile lessened a little of the sting. That mouth… He was a huge fan of it. Some guys called themselves leg men and Reid had always thought that sort of attitude was so limiting when a woman had many attributes worth praising. But he got it now. When she smiled, he felt it in his gut. He was officially a mouth man.

"Well," she murmured, smoothing a finger over one of his knuckles. "Maybe *moping* isn't the right word but you're doing something. Carrying around a lot of guilt over the plane crash and what came after, I guess. Would Sophia be angry with you for how it turned out? If she was standing in front of you right now, would she punch you in the face and tell you that you're a crappy brother?"

"Maybe." When Nora's brows snapped together in frustration, he shrugged. "Maybe not. I think she'd approve of Gina. It doesn't make me any better of a person."

It also didn't make him any less selfish or any more of the kind of guy who could be a dad. A woman like Nora wasn't for him for a lot of reasons. She deserved better. She'd skipped right over that piece of the puzzle and nothing she said could change that.

"You can't think like that."

"Like what? That it's my fault?" He shook his head with a dark, unamused chuckle. "But it is. I could have done something. I could have saved Sophia and my mom. If only I'd been there instead of at the Metropol."

What had been his passion had become his refuge. The place he hid from his crimes. The world seemed to be spinning on without him, so obviously he'd made a good decision for once to remove himself from polite society.

Sympathy flooded Nora's gaze, weighted her touch as she squeezed his fingers. "Or you could have died along with them. Also fate. Because if you had, you wouldn't be here now. With me."

Something shifted in the atmosphere as they stared at each other.

"No. I wouldn't be." But he wasn't so sure that was a good thing. While he'd hoped she'd accept his apology and then perhaps they could move on to more intimate activities, he hadn't expected that she'd uncover all his raw places with her understanding and pointed questions. "I should go."

"Don't you dare run away." Her grip tightened on his hand, pinning it to the leather cushion. "We're just getting started. I'm happy you're here, in case that wasn't abundantly clear. I don't get out much. I haven't been on a date since before Sean was deployed over two years ago. I'm enjoying this."

"You're…enjoying this? Which part? When I made you cry or when I admitted how I put my company ahead of my family? I'm a selfish workaholic who can never be a father, which means you should kick me out before I hurt you, too."

A noise of disgust burst from her throat. "Stop it. You say that like working a lot automatically makes you a bad father. Declan's dad was stationed overseas. How often do you think they would have seen each other? But we had a plan to make it work. That's what you do when you have kids. You improvise. Compromise. Figure things out. Because they're so worth it."

Nora's face had taken on a sharp, sweet expression as she talked about her son. *That's* what was missing, what Reid's DNA had skipped over when building his soul. Reid had never felt that way about Sophia's children. They were cute, sure. But he didn't love them unconditionally, the way Nora obviously felt about Declan. Sacrifice wasn't in his tool kit.

"I'm not father material," he said.

She needed to understand this before anything else

happened between them. She could spin his decisions in a way that made it seem like forgiveness might be possible, but there was no happily-ever-after where he filled in the holes of her and Declan's lives.

"You underestimate yourself," she countered. "When it matters, you find a way to be more than you ever thought you could."

"Chamberlain Group comes first," he said flatly. Brutally. "I have no desire to be a father and so I didn't become one, nor do I plan to ever do so. That's why I don't date women with children. Where could it possibly go?"

Nora's mouth flattened. "You might as well say you don't date women *without* children, either, because all of them might someday want to have one, so you're out from the get-go."

That was one of his worst fears. "Fair enough. Then it might be better to describe my current state by saying I don't typically date anyone."

"Except me."

He nodded. "You are the exception in more ways than one."

"That seems quite implausible given your *reputation*. It may not be one hundred percent true but the rumors have to start somewhere." She couldn't have infused more innuendo into the statement if she'd tried. If he didn't miss his guess, the whole idea intrigued her.

Normally, the subject of his prowess in the bedroom pissed him off because it almost always came from uninformed gossipmongers who latched onto a titillating topic in hopes of spicing up their own boring lives.

With Nora, it might well be an opportunity to push the boundaries with a willing partner whom he already knew how to play like a well-tuned piano. The whole idea intrigued *him*, as well. Against all reason.

"Make no mistake." He caught her chin with his palm and guided it upward in order to meet her gaze. She didn't balk, staring him down without blinking, making him think that her spirit might be his favorite thing about her. "I have plenty of sex. A few hours of pleasure now and again is one of life's basic necessities. But I always make sure my lovers know the score and I rarely come back for seconds."

A saucy smile bloomed on her face. "So you being here tonight. Is that considered seconds?"

"Yes. And thirds."

Heat gathered in her expression as she absorbed that. Awareness built on itself, stretching the moment into a charged encounter that shouldn't have aroused him as much as it did. At least not so fast. But his body reacted of its own accord. He had a hell of an erection even as his pulse raced double time.

"I'll consider myself schooled on the score, then," she murmured. "Full disclosure. I'm not looking for anything more than a few hours of pleasure. I'm going back to Colorado soon and I won't be coming back to Chicago. Tonight, you need me. I need you. There's nothing more complicated about us than that."

So it seemed as if he'd freaked out over nothing. And now he felt like whacking himself in the head with a hammer. He'd missed out on the culmination of his dinner with Nora the other night over his own stupidity. A hot, willing woman had surrendered herself to wherever the mood took them and he'd *kicked her out*.

Being alone suited him. Mostly. Tonight it felt right to be with Nora.

When Nora had expressed a desire to better understand this complex man, she'd never dreamed she'd get her wish in such a deep and irrevocable fashion. The pain radiating from his beautiful brown eyes… It was almost too much for her to bear. Too much for her to internalize.

Because she identified with it far more easily than she wanted.

"You need me?" he repeated.

So much.

"Yes." The answer floated from her throat on a whisper. "You're not the only one who's still dealing with loss."

Wordlessly, he held out his hand and she took it. The contact sang through her, vibrating along all her nerve endings. The moment stretched as they shared a near-spiritual sense of unity. *Connection.* It had been present almost from the first but she hadn't recognized it for what it was: two souls finding each other, finding what they'd both so desperately sought. Someone to ease the pain and loneliness.

It was so much more than reconnecting with an old friend. Because neither of them was the same person as before. That was okay. Tonight, they had connected on a whole new level.

The way Reid was looking at her was…*delicious*. Nora let the feeling flow all the way down into her core, where it burst open in a heated shower of desire.

She should have been ashamed. She'd never dreamed she'd be the kind of woman who could indulge in a wicked encounter with a man she had no intention of marrying, no desire to fall in love with and no plans to even see again. But she'd not only already done that the other night, her body was gearing up to do it again.

Except when Reid reached out, cupping her cheek with one hand, his touch blew that lie to pieces. This wasn't a one-night stand with an anonymous man. It was *Reid*. As she absorbed his heat, the hugeness of what he'd shared settled over her. *She needed him*—to salve her own loneliness, to feel alive. To connect with him on a higher level than just over mutual pain.

She wanted to connect through mutual pleasure. And afterward, to know they'd helped each other heal in some small way. They had no future together, but what they experienced tonight might change their individual futures. Oh, she genuinely hoped it would.

Reid's curls begged for her fingers so she reached out to sink her fingers into them all the way to the knuckle.

The moment she touched him, he came alive, reaching back, yanking her into his arms. Their lips met hungrily, without hesitation. His essence spilled into her as he kissed her. Filling her. Beating back the weight of life as together, they experienced something good and wonderful.

They both deserved the peace to be found only in each other's arms.

Except, in her mind, the pleasure scale remained completely unbalanced. She owed him one unbelievable, mind-blowing orgasm, the kind he'd dream about for several nights to come.

Masterfully, he gripped her jaw and shifted her to take the kiss deeper. His powerful, thrilling tongue worked its way farther into her mouth to claim hers, taste it. Heat engulfed her, radiating along her skin, diving under it to boil her blood. Her pulse hammered as his hand snaked under her T-shirt to fan across her bare back.

She was drowning in him, in the sensations of his hands on her flesh, his lips on hers. Who was doing the giving here?

Before he stole her ability to think completely, she pulled away and threw one leg over his lap to straddle him and...*oh*. His hard length nudged her core and he gazed at her without speaking, his eyes hot and heavy-lidded with desire. For her.

"Better," she murmured.

His hands settled at her waist and he pulled, grinding her harder against his erection. Sparks burst at the contact point and her head tipped back automatically.

"It's getting there," he growled, and fused his lips to her throat.

First he nibbled, then sucked hard on the tender skin at her neck. There would be marks in the morning. Good. She wanted this man's brand on her body. A physical reminder that they'd shared something.

But she wasn't ready to surrender to him, to the sensations she knew were in store for her at his hands. Somehow, she pulled his mouth from the hollow of her neck and forcefully manacled his wrists, pinning them to the couch on either side of his shoulders.

"You. Be still."

His brows rose. "Because why?"

"The other night, I was the star of the show. You were behind me and I couldn't see you in the window. This time, it's your turn. "

Intrigue filled his expression. "I'm dying to find out what that means. And how you're going to stop me from touching you as much as I please."

Challenge accepted.

Seven

Nora contemplated the man at her complete mercy. Of course, that state of affairs would last only as long as it amused him to allow such a thing. She had no illusions about whether or not he could break free of her hands if he wanted to.

But he wouldn't.

"You're going to do exactly as I say and like it," she instructed, rolling her hips forward to notch his erection deeper into her recesses. Exactly where she wanted it most. "I've had precious few things I can control in my life lately. If I say you don't get to touch me, you'll obey because you want me to be happy."

"Yes," he murmured, his voice thick with passion

"FAST FIVE" READER SURVEY

Your participation entitles you to:
✳ **4 Thank-You Gifts Worth Over $20!**

Complete the survey in minutes.

Get **2 FREE** Books

Your Thank-You Gifts include **2 FREE BOOKS** and **2 MYSTERY GIFTS**. There's no obligation to purchase anything!

See inside for details.

Please help make our
"Fast Five" Reader Survey
a success!

Dear Reader,

Since you are a lover of our books, your opinions are important to us... and so is your time.

That's why we made sure your **"FAST FIVE" READER SURVEY** can be completed in just a few minutes. Your answers to the five questions will help us remain at the forefront of women's fiction.

And, as a thank-you for participating, we'd like to send you **4 FREE THANK-YOU GIFTS!**

Enjoy your gifts with our appreciation,

Pam Powers

that made her shiver. "I do want you to be happy. What would you like me to do, then?"

It was a total turn-on to have his agreement, to have complete control over a man's body, especially one as powerful and commanding as Reid Chamberlain's. Especially one she'd dreamed about as a teenager. Of course, her harmless young fantasies had included a kiss under the mistletoe hanging from the center arch at her parents' house one Christmas. Or holding hands at a football game.

Having permission to do whatever she wanted to a man who had grown up to be sinfully gorgeous and masculine, one who had gained a reputation for unusual tastes, was a far cry from that.

It should frighten her. It didn't.

"Let me undress you," she said.

Bold, decisive. She liked it.

He held out his hands in surrender, one to each side, and she watched him as she worked on the first button. It popped free and she traced a line down his torso to the next one, delighting in the feel of his crisp chest hair against her fingertip.

His eyelids shuttered as she touched him, and that was a turn-on, too. She'd barely gotten started and she'd already pleased him. And there was more where that came from.

She spread his shirt wide, drinking in the curves and valleys of his well-defined chest, sucking in her murmur of appreciation because it sounded childish to be so impressed by a man's physique. But he was gorgeous, muscled and bronzed, as if he'd spent hours honing his body strictly for her viewing pleasure.

"I like it when you look at me," he told her unnecessarily. She could feel the evidence between her legs as his hips strained forward, seeking her hungrily.

What else might he like? She had precious little experience with men other than the one she'd been married to. Sure, they'd had a good relationship in the bedroom, but this was different.

Reid was different. And that meant she could be different, too. This was her chance to be as experimental as she wished, with no fear of judgment. No worries about where their relationship was going, whether he'd be good for Declan, none of that. Because this was one night only.

There were no rules.

It was freeing and exciting.

Pulling him forward by his shirt, she dived into a kiss with gusto.

Instantly, his hard lips softened under hers as he surrendered to her completely, allowing her to explore to her heart's content. She traced the line of his closed mouth, forcing her tongue inside, opening him wide so she could taste him. Wine and man melded together, delicious and tempting at the same time.

More. She deepened the kiss, drawing a groan from him that vibrated against her breasts. Her nipples hardened under her bra, aching to be free of the confines of her clothes. *Not yet.* This initial round was about Reid and his pleasure. Not hers.

Going on instinct alone, she broke off the kiss and yanked his shirt free from his arms, then slid to the floor between his legs. He watched her as she unbuckled his belt, and the unbanked fire raging in his gaze turned her fingers numb. Somehow she got the leather strap untangled and pulled, then worked on the button and zipper holding his pants closed.

His erection strained against the fabric and she accidentally grazed it with her fingernails. He sucked in a strangled breath, and that's when her nerves completely disappeared.

This was his turn. She had the power to make him come and she planned to.

Slowly, she drew down the zipper and then hooked the waistband of his briefs with her forefingers to slide them down just a bit, just enough. His erection sprang free, gorgeous and thick, and so close to her mouth she couldn't resist a small taste.

It pulsed under her tongue. She wrapped one hand around the base to hold him still as she took the rest between her lips. Groaning, he slid a hand to the back of her neck, holding her head in place, which thrilled her. She shut her eyes, concentrating on the flesh filling her mouth as she sucked.

His hips bucked, driving him deeper, and she worked him relentlessly, shamelessly, until he froze and uttered a guttural expletive, then came in a glorious, salty burst that left her quite pleased with herself.

She cleaned up, giving him a few minutes to collect himself, and then she settled back into a spot near him on the couch. "That was amazing."

His brown eyes filled with amusement. "I think that's my line."

Still no smile. She'd have to work on that. "Let me know when you're rested up. I've got a few more things on the agenda."

"I'm done."

Lightning quick, he hauled her into his arms and devoured her whole from the inside out with nothing more than a kiss. Lips burning against hers, his tongue demanded entry. Heat skidded across her skin as he swirled into her mouth, flesh on flesh. Relentlessly, he deepened the kiss again and again, winding his fingers through her hair to slowly draw her head backward until she was helplessly caught in his powerful embrace.

His mouth raced down her throat and cool air caressed her bare skin an instant before she realized he'd yanked her shirt and bra strap down to reveal one shoulder. The bite of his teeth as they sank into her flesh made her flinch, but then he rested the palm of his hand against her shoulder blade, soothing her as he held her in place, pleasuring her with his whole mouth.

And it was pleasurable. She had never thought her shoulder could be an erogenous zone, but she wouldn't make that mistake again. Moaning, she leaned into his lips as his tongue laved over the spot where he'd nibbled, which still smarted a bit. It was an intense experience. Unique. Much like watching herself come the other night.

The memory blasted through her, dampening the juncture between her legs. Desperate for relief, she rolled her hips against the crease of her jeans but it wasn't enough.

Reid paused long enough to notice her discomfort and with a wicked gleam in his eye, he sat back. "Don't forget, your wish is my command."

How *could* she have forgotten? If she wanted him to touch her, all she had to do was say so. With two fingers, she flicked open the button of her jeans and unzipped them. Wiggling free of her panties at the same time, she lay back on the couch. "I want that mouth on me. Here."

She rested a hand on her mound. His trademark ghost of a smile curved his lips as he swept her with a heated glance.

Wordlessly, he put a hand on each knee and pushed, opening her up. And then…she bucked as his tongue connected with her center. A thick wave of pleasure radiated outward to engulf her whole body.

Those gorgeous lips nibbled at her flesh at the same moment he plunged his fingers into her core. Again. Deeper. He twisted his fingers inside her. Sucked at her. Higher and higher she soared as his talented mouth treated her to the hottest experience of her life.

When she came, she thrust her hips upward against his mouth and he bit down. Lightly, but enough that she felt it. The combination of sensations ripped through her, and she cried out as her vision dimmed.

Reid's fingers drew out the orgasm, draining her. Filling her. His mouth on her was the sweetest paradox. They were fully connected, yet not. She wanted more.

"Take me to your bed," he demanded hoarsely before she'd fully recovered. "I need to be inside you."

She needed that, too. *Now.*

Urgency Reid didn't recognize coiled low in his belly as he scooped up the still-quivering woman from the couch and carried her across the room. He followed Nora's breathless directions until he found the bed. Gently, he laid her out on the coverlet, fished two condoms from his back pocket and stripped.

She watched him, her gaze sensual and expectant.

With reverence, he sat her up so he could remove her T-shirt. They had a bad habit of getting way too hot, way too fast, and clothes seemed to be the least of their concerns.

No more. He wanted to see her. The creamy swell of her breasts fell loose as he unhooked her bra and he couldn't stop himself from thumbing one nipple. It felt like silk. He fondled the other one in kind and she arched her back, moaning as he circled them, squeezing gently.

"Reid," she gasped.

"Yes? Something you want?"

"You."

Nonsensical sounds poured from her throat as he sucked a pert, hard nipple into his mouth. Heaven. He rolled the tip along the ridges of his teeth. She liked it when he got a little rough, as evidenced yet again when she shifted against his lips, shoving her nipple deeper into his mouth. He liked obliging her. Her responses to the slightest bite…unbelievable.

He couldn't wait to see what else she'd like.

On a whim, he flipped her over and drew her up on her knees, shoulders down against the coverlet, her legs spread wide to reveal all her secrets.

"I want to see you," he murmured and knelt between her thighs to trace his tongue along the crease he'd so thoroughly acquainted himself with mere moments ago. But then he'd been focused on pleasuring her. This perusal was purely for his own benefit.

And it was hot. So hot, his erection flared to life again. Faster than he'd have anticipated.

Her hips rocked, pressing her folds against his mouth, and he indulged her by driving his tongue straight into her wet center. She filled his taste buds and he fingered her bud until her head was thrashing against the coverlet.

Nora was so wet for him. It was the most arousing taste he'd ever had.

"Reid, please," she sobbed, and as he was about

to lose his mind anyway, he rolled on a condom and gripped her hips.

She was so gorgeous spread out like this. Her backside was legendary, lush. He watched as his tip nudged her entrance from behind and then he sank into her slick, tight center. Instantly, she accepted him to the hilt and she gasped as he held her in place, savoring the feel. Slowly, he withdrew and plunged in again, and the angle was amazing.

She was amazing.

Something snapped in his chest and spilled warmth all over him. But it wasn't the heat of lust. It was something else, and his frozen, dark places evaporated as if they'd never existed. There was only Nora.

Watching them joined like this... The image heightened the urgency of his lovemaking. He couldn't hold back and didn't have to. She met his hard, quick thrusts and then some. They came together again and again until they both cried out in tandem. As she closed around him like a snug fist, he emptied himself.

He snaked an arm around her chest and rolled, taking them both to the mattress, her hot body spooned tight against his.

He didn't let go. Might never let go. His torso heaved against her spine. Spent, he lay there unable to move, unable to collect his scattered thoughts.

How did they top *that*?

Of course, the beauty of it was that they didn't have

to. He could leave and never call her again. A few hours of pleasure had been delivered, as specified.

He didn't pull away, jam his legs into his pants and scout for the exit as he had so many times in the past. Instead, he pressed his lips to Nora's temple and pulled her closer, still inside her and not the slightest bit interested in changing that. He should be. He should leave. She snuggled deeper underneath his arm, and he couldn't have pulled away if his life depended on it.

"I have another bottle of wine," she murmured. "And several chick flicks bookmarked on Netflix. Wanna watch *Bridget Jones's Diary* with me?"

"Sure." That was a mistake. What the hell was he doing agreeing to stick around?

"Really?" She half rolled and eyed him over her shoulder as if he'd started speaking Swahili. "*Bridget Jones* isn't the kind of thing men usually go for."

He cursed. She'd expected him to leave, too. They weren't a couple who lay around post-sex and had wine, falling asleep in each other's arms. She'd probably just offered out of courtesy.

Smooth, Chamberlain. "Maybe I should take a rain check. Early meeting."

Her face fell. "Oh. I was looking forward to it. Grace and Eve canceled on me and, well… Never mind. We agreed this was—"

Capturing her wide, unsmiling mouth, he kissed her nonsense away. "Forget I mentioned anything about a rain check. I'll get the wine. You get the movie."

"Okay. Let me check on Declan. Back in a flash."

And that was how he found himself wrapped up in Nora, sitting up against pillows in her bed, watching a movie about a British woman played by an actress he'd swear wasn't British. But Nora laughed every so often, and it thrummed through his torso in a thoroughly pleasant way. He'd do it again in a heartbeat.

When the credits rolled, Nora glanced up at him. "This is the best date I've ever had."

At her sweet admission, something unfolded inside him, and he didn't know what to do with it. This had been a date? He had precious little to compare it with, but she'd been married, which meant she'd probably gone on a lot of dates with the guy she'd eventually tied the knot with. What had Reid done that was so much better?

"You need to get out more."

"Or less." She snuggled up against his chest and his arms tightened involuntarily. "I'm not a fan of crowds. Staying in like this is perfect. It's exactly what I needed."

It suited him, as well. She fit him far better than he'd have guessed. The sex had been off the charts. No holds barred. Meaningful, when it shouldn't have been.

But that didn't change facts. The evening had been the best date of his life, too.

Too bad they weren't dating. "I should go."

She sat up. "You keep saying that. And then not

doing it. In case there's any confusion, I'd be more than happy if you stayed the night."

As in *all night*? His throat pinched with something that felt a lot like panic. "That's not really my thing."

"Trust me, it's not my typical thing, either. But…" She trailed off, looking so frustrated and forlorn that he couldn't stand it.

Tipping her chin up, he forced her to meet his gaze. "What is it?"

"I just don't want to be alone. Not after the spectacular evening we've had so far." She crossed her arms over her stomach, vulnerability practically bleeding from her pores. "Stay."

"I'm not going anywhere."

The instant he said it, he wished he could take it back. What the hell was wrong with him? It was as if his brain and his vocal cords had never met. They certainly weren't on the same page.

But then she smiled and he forgot why it was a bad idea to stay. She didn't want to be alone and for the first time in a long time, neither did he. At least until she fell asleep. Then he could dash for the door without her being the wiser.

He pulled her back into his arms, content to just be with her, for now. Who could blame him, when the scent of vanilla and strawberries and sex lingered in the air? She was just as sweet dozing against his chest as she had been against his tongue when he pleasured her. He almost hated to leave. But he had to. That way, there would be no morning after, no opportunity for regret, for what-ifs, for *maybe we should think about a second date...*

Just one night. And it was over.

Reid turned off the TV and settled Nora's head against the pillow as he eased out from under her. She shifted, drawing her palm up to rest a cheek on it, but she didn't wake. He pulled the covers up over her naked form, hiding the faint marks on her shoulder and neck.

What they'd done behind closed doors was private. And he liked that he'd left her with something of a re-minder that would fade into memory, just like their night together.

Which was over, he reminded himself yet again. Why was he still standing here soaking up the gor-geous vision of Nora sleeping in her bed, replete from his lovemaking? Because he wanted to curl up next to her again. Wake up with her in the morning and do it all over again.

That wasn't the deal. Nor was the deal open to alter-ation. It wasn't as though he'd had to talk her into one night only. She'd been the one to insist on that, which fit him to a T.

Reid went out into the living room and found his pants, underwear and shirt, but his belt was nowhere to be seen. Glancing back toward the hall that led to Nora's bedroom, he risked turning on the light in hopes of locating it.

"Mmmair. Mmmair."

What the hell was that? Reid's hand froze on the light switch he'd just flipped.

He whipped around. A tiny redheaded boy dressed in pajamas with a picture of a dinosaur on the chest stood in the dead center of the living room. Looking at him.

Reid's pulse jumped. "Um, hi."

Declan. Obviously. Reid did a mental sweep for the information he'd gleaned from Nora about her son. He liked books and blankets and was…how old? Two? Wasn't the kid too little to be wandering around in an unfamiliar house at night? By himself?

"Mmmair."

"Hey, buddy. You go on back to bed. Nothing to see here."

Not one muscle in the boy's body moved. Now what? Reid edged toward the door, eyeing it. Couldn't he still just leave? An ocean of Oriental carpet stretched between him and freedom. One small twist of the doorknob and he could—

"Mmmair."

Reid sighed. He'd be frustrated by the lack of communication, but Nora had probably drilled "Stranger Danger" into her son's head so well that he wasn't about to talk to some unfamiliar man who happened to be present in the living room at—Reid glanced at the clock on the mantel—1:45 a.m.

That's when Reid noticed the boy had tears welling up in his eyes. He cursed and then nearly bit off his tongue. You weren't supposed to talk like that around kids.

"What's wrong...Declan?"

Maybe if he called him by name, it would ease some of the tension, most of which seemed to be in Reid's legs, weighing them down. Rooting him to the spot. He couldn't leave, not now. Not in the middle of whatever crisis was going on with Nora's son. Besides, Reid couldn't walk out the door until he could be sure Declan wouldn't follow him outside or turn on the oven or order an X-rated movie with the universal remote lying on the couch.

The door was so close, and yet so far.

"Mmmair. Mmmair," Declan insisted, the tears spilling down his little face.

Nora. Nora could fix this. The kid obviously needed his mom, who could interpret this foreign, little-boy language with practiced ease.

But she was asleep. If Reid woke her up, there would be a whole...thing about whether he was going to stay the night. He couldn't do that, no matter how much he inexplicably wanted to. It wasn't fair to anyone.

Reid glanced at the door and then back at the hallway where Declan had come from. "Let's find your room, okay? We can handle that."

Wonder of wonders, Declan nodded. But he didn't move. Cautiously, Reid approached him the way he would a feral dog: hand outstretched, lots of eye contact and soothing noises.

The kid watched him unflinchingly. The moment

Reid got within two feet, Declan's little arms stretched out and latched onto Reid's leg. Tight. Like a barnacle.

Oh, hell no. Reid groaned. What was he supposed to do now?

"Come on, kid. Give me a break," he muttered, wondering if it was okay to pry him off.

But he might hurt Declan. He had literally never touched a child in his life. Okay, well, not as an adult. He'd punched Nash plenty of times when they were growing up. But that was different. They'd been pretty close to the same size at the time.

Reid shook his leg. Gently. Declan did not magically detach.

"Declan." Reid waited until he looked up, and then spoke to him as he would anyone else who was being unreasonable. "You have to let go or I won't be able to walk."

Actually, that wasn't entirely true, as Reid discovered when he dragged his leg toward the hall—and Declan moved with him. So that was the secret. Reid shuffled. Declan shuffled. Eventually they got halfway down the hall, where Reid paused to get his bearings.

Which one was the kid's room? Nora's was at the end of the hall, as Reid well knew, but he'd failed to do an inventory of the rest of the house since it had never occurred to him that he'd be scouting for a place to deposit a two-year-old with stickier arms than an octopus.

Faint light spilled from one of the open doors. That seemed like a good candidate.

Reid did a few more shuffle-drag steps and peered inside the room. A white crib sat against one wall, with an antique writing desk against the adjacent wall. The floor was covered with a patchwork quilt sporting blobby animal shapes, and a night-light glowed from one of the plugs.

It looked as if the room had been repurposed for the little boy, but he didn't immediately untangle himself and toddle inside the way Reid had hoped.

"Here's your room, Declan," Reid whispered, ever mindful of Nora's open door not too far down the hall.

Declan tightened his arms. *Okay, then.* Looked like he was all in. Reid dragged Declan into the room and closed the door. "We'll just have us some men time, then."

Reid eased down onto the quilt. The moment his butt hit the ground, Declan's did, too, and he finally released his death grip. And he wasn't crying. So it was a win all the way around.

"Maybe we can get back in bed?" Reid suggested casually, eyeing the crib. How did one maneuver such a contraption? Clearly Declan had gotten out of it. Did he know how to get back in by himself?

This would be one of those times when it would be beneficial to have a manual. Reid fished his phone from his pocket and googled "How to put a baby in a crib."

Holy crap. An ungodly number of results appeared on the screen. But as he scrolled through them, most seemed to be about keeping the kid there once you got him into the thing.

"Yeah, already figured out that was a problem," he told his phone sarcastically as he thumbed past "15 Tips to Help Your Child Sleep through the Night."

Declan crawled over and peered at the screen with his head cocked, and then promptly plopped into Reid's lap, as if they'd done this a hundred times.

Reid groaned. The boy had put all his weight right on Reid's ankle bone. No problem. He could stand it. Probably. The seconds ticked by as together, they knocked out this task of reading useless articles debating the benefits of laying a baby on his back, stomach or side.

Nora's son wasn't even in the bed yet. How to position him on the mattress didn't matter a hell of a lot at this point in time.

Reid's leg started tingling. There was no helping it. He had to shift the child's weight. Dropping his phone, he gingerly gripped Declan's upper arms and pulled up, resituating his own legs, the boy's legs, and trying whatever else could be done with what felt like a fifty-pound sack of potatoes in his grip.

And then somehow, the boy half squirmed, half rolled and ended up cradled in Reid's arms. Huh. He'd have sworn Declan was too big to fit like this, but there you go. It seemed like a good next step would be standing and maybe he could ease the boy into his crib.

Should have thought of that, moron. What a simple solution.

Reid stood. Apparently he owed his personal trainer an apology for cursing the man out for the last three months over that exercise designed to hone his glutes. Reid hated that exercise. But it had worked.

He carried Declan to the crib and eased him onto the mattress. Maybe Reid should have actually paid attention to the article on the pros and cons of putting a baby on his stomach or back because hell if he knew whether this was the right way to do it.

Declan rolled and stood up, hands gripping the side of the crib. "Mmmair."

And...never mind. Reid sighed. "Seriously? Come on, lie back down. Please."

"Mmmair."

"What does that even mean?" Frustrated, Reid scowled at Declan. "Is that the name of your stuffed animal or something?"

Declan threw a leg over the side of the crib, clearly intent on repeating his escape.

"Oh, no. Not that again." Reid pushed back on Declan's leg and pointed to the mattress. "We're in the bed. We're not getting out until morning."

Which would be here much sooner than Reid would like, at this rate. If he didn't get this sorted out, he and Nora would be having a lovely conversation over coffee about how Reid had been the go-to substitute daddy during the night.

Ice coated Reid's lungs and they refused to fill with air. He wasn't father material. He'd told Nora this. And this situation was a case in point. Maybe Reid should just pretend he'd never heard Declan and get out while the getting was still good.

Declan stuck two fingers in his mouth. "Mmmair."

For whatever reason, the word sounded different than the other nine hundred times the boy had uttered it. Different enough that it was suddenly a word that had meaning. Reid frowned. "Did you have a nightmare?"

Two tears flung loose from Declan's face as he nodded. Progress. Except now everything was so much worse. A *nightmare*. As Reid had experienced his fair share of those, he fully sympathized. Poor kid. Only a heartless bastard would walk away after that kind of brave confession.

And while Reid would have labeled himself exactly that every day of the week and twice on Sunday...that little tear-filled face stabbed at something inside and there was no other recourse than to work through his reluctance. But what was Reid supposed to do?

Before he could think twice, Reid scooped the kid from his prison and stretched out on the floor, situating Declan near him on the patchwork quilt. His elbow landed somewhere in the middle of an elephant as he propped his head up on his hand.

Somehow, the words to a long-forgotten song filtered through his head. A song his mother had sung to him when he was young. Soon Reid found himself singing and stroking Declan's back. The way his own mom had done.

His throat seized up, cutting off the song midhum.

God, he missed his mother. She'd had her flaws but she'd loved Reid unconditionally and he'd forgotten what that felt like. Here on the floor with no one else but a near-mute little boy as his only witness, he let the memories flow and didn't check his monumental grief as he normally did.

Acute sadness welled up in him. It was almost too much to bear. He had to get out of here before he became a blubbery mess. Besides, memories of his mother came part and parcel with memories of his father... which reminded Reid all over again what lurked in his DNA.

Darkness. Maybe even a deeper brand than Reid had already experienced. What if *becoming* a father brought out the worst traits of his bloodline and he found out too late? He should leave for that reason alone. No one under this roof deserved to be subjected to the murderous, suicidal tendencies that had lurked in his father's soul and surely lurked in Reid's, too.

But he forced himself to lie there with Declan until the boy fell still, his lashes flat against his cheeks and his chest rising and falling rhythmically. Surely the boy could sleep here on the floor, right? There was no way Reid could put him back in that crib, not with how clearly Declan had expressed his preference to be out of it. He'd probably wake up and climb back out again anyway.

Now he could leave with a clear conscience.

As Reid ducked out the door, he breathed deeply for the first time in what felt like a million years. It had been pure beginner's luck and only his intense desire to let Nora sleep had motivated him to succeed. No way could Reid ever deal with something like that again. It was way too intense.

Eight

What in the world?

Nora pushed open the door of Declan's room. It had been wide open when she checked on him last night before watching the movie with Reid. She always left it open so she could hear him if he called for her in the middle of the night.

Declan lay on the floor in the middle of his quilt, head pillowed on one chubby arm. Asleep.

Hands on her hips, her pulse hammering in her throat, Nora watched her son sleep. He'd started climbing out of his crib at home a couple of weeks ago but then he'd stopped and she'd—wrongly—assumed he'd had his fun doing it, then lost interest.

Guess not. He must have closed the door but how he'd

done so without waking her up was baffling. It wasn't as though he could reach the doorknob, so he'd have to have pushed it shut. But she hadn't heard it, and her razor-sharp hearing had never failed her.

Good thing he hadn't come into her room last night.

Her cheeks warmed. Yeah, some of that might have traumatized Declan for life. And wouldn't that have been a disaster if Declan had run into Reid. One sight of her pint-size wonder would have sent Reid screaming for the hills.

No matter. Reid must have left well before Declan had performed his Houdini act. And that was perfect. Exactly as she'd expected. Their one night was over and she had several great memories to keep her warm for a good long while. Yeah, the sex had been *wow* and then some. No surprise there. But the way he'd made her feel…treasured. Beautiful. Exciting. That had been totally unexpected. Wonderful. Reid Chamberlain was so much more than a talented lover.

And if she'd been a little sad when she woke up and realized Reid had already left—without saying goodbye—no one had to know. She'd take that secret to the grave. She shouldn't have asked him to stay in the first place and she appreciated that Reid had figured out a way to let her save face, but not give in. Waking up together would have opened up their relationship to further speculation and there was nothing to speculate about.

Declan's eyes blinked open. "Daadee."

"What's that?"

Her son had added a new word to his vocabulary apparently. She loved the discovery process, where she got a chance to learn more about what went on in his head and communicate with this amazing little creature she'd been gifted with.

"Daadee."

"Daddy? Oh, honey." Nora shut her eyes for a blink. That was the one word she'd dreaded him learning. "Your daddy is in heaven. It's just you and me now."

A travesty. And what she wouldn't give for it to be different. But it was the cold, hard truth. If she'd loved Sean a little less or wasn't so worried about Declan being hurt by future loss, she might consider dating a nice man who could eventually fill that daddy-shaped hole in her son's heart.

After all, Declan would know Sean only from pictures. He'd never be held by his father or play baseball with his dad cheering on the sidelines. Nora had no doubt there were men out there who could love a kid who wasn't their blood. She just didn't have any interest in opening herself or her kid up for anything less than a sure thing. Which didn't exist. The odds favored an eventual breakup, more loss, more tragedy. Something other than a happily-ever-after—because that was Nora's reality.

"Daadee," Declan repeated and pointed at the door.

"Sorry, Butterbean. There's no daddy on the other side of that door."

Declan took it upon himself to make sure, doing a

thorough search of the whole guesthouse, while Nora followed him, perplexed by his dogged determination. It rubbed at her the wrong way. Something had to have jump-started all of this.

Had Declan caught a glimpse of Reid last night and let his little-boy imagination go wild? Surely not. But then Nora hadn't ever brought a man around Declan. What if he had seen his mother kissing a man? Maybe he'd latched onto the idea of having a daddy of his own.

Nora's heart nearly squeezed out of her chest as Declan gave up his mysterious quest, finally plopping down on the Oriental carpet in front of the TV with a frustrated scowl. He refused to eat breakfast, refused the stuffed animals Nora tried to entertain him with, refused to watch any of his favorite shows. It was like trying to deal with a brick wall.

By 10:00 a.m., Nora was ready to pull her hair out. Her sisters had called from the hospital twice, wondering where Nora was. She'd intended to go by this morning but all the daddy talk had sidetracked her time frame.

"Okay, Butterbean. Enough with the theatrics. We're going to see Grandpa and you're going to be on your best behavior." Which was a little like telling the wind where to blow. Fruitless.

Somehow she got Mr. Impossible into the town car Eve had sent and buckled him into the car seat. Declan clutched a baggie of banana chips in lieu of breakfast, but it was food, so Nora considered it a victory.

The Chicago skyline unfolded outside the window and she was a little ashamed her eye shot straight to the twisted tower near the north end—the Metropol. Reid was inside the building somewhere. Was he thinking about their night together, remembering how amazing it was?

If so, that made two of them.

She shouldn't be thinking about him at all. He'd made it clear there was no future for them. If there was anyone more ill-suited to being that nice man who could fill the holes in her life, it was Reid Chamberlain.

Holes in *Declan's* life, she'd meant. Her own life had no holes. It was full of motherhood and dealing with her father's health problems. While she would go home eventually, she might have fudged the time frame with Reid a little bit, making it sound like she'd be jetting off in a few days, when she'd really planned to be in Chicago for the foreseeable future.

Her father was dying. She'd never forgive herself if she left without reconciling with him.

When Nora entered her father's hospital room, his eyes shifted toward her but otherwise, he didn't move.

"Hi, Dad."

Gaunt and pale, her father looked twenty years older than the picture she carried of him in her head. Cancer had aged him and it was a visual reminder that it would eventually kill him. Grief sloshed through Nora's stomach over the years of pain this man had caused. She'd missed out on having a loving father. Her son would, too, a commonality she mourned, but she'd had no control over the circumstances of Sean's death.

Sutton had made his own choices that prevented Nora's childhood from being the one she'd imagined other children getting to have. And some of those choices would prevent her son from knowing his grandfather. Some widows had supportive fathers who stepped into the gaping hole where their husbands used to be. Nora wasn't one of them.

"Nora." Her father's voice had degenerated into a gravelly growl, but it still carried a sense of authority. "You're late."

There were so many things she wanted to say in response to that, but none of them were conducive to reconciliation. So she smiled instead because that was what she did best: pretend everything was fine.

She chatted *at* her dad, not with him, because letting him get a word in edgewise gave him too much of an opening to say something horrible, mean or manipulative. Or all three. She told him about the modest house she lived in and the small town of Silver Falls that she'd moved to after Sean died because she couldn't stand living in Colorado Springs anymore, where the memories were sharpest.

Declan climbed up on Nora's lap to peer at his grandfather. "Pa."

"You may call me Grandfather," Sutton informed the boy, his brows snapping together. "Or you may refrain from addressing me."

Apparently, when correcting someone, her father had plenty of energy.

"For crying out loud, Dad. Declan is barely two." Nora stood, hauling Declan up against her hip, which got harder every day since Declan grew like a weed. "Since both of us lack the ability to meet your exacting standards, we'll do you the courtesy of removing ourselves from your presence."

Shaking so hard she feared she'd drop Declan, Nora fled the hospital room, nearly plowing into Eve outside the door.

"Where are you going?" she asked with a frown. "You've only been here for an hour."

"Don't start."

But Nora felt guilty and wondered if she'd been too hasty in dashing out of her father's hospital room. Either she wanted to reconcile—which meant accepting her father as is, poisonous personality and all—or she had to wash her hands of him.

Neither option made her feel like bursting into song Rodgers and Hammerstein–style right there in hospital corridor. She sighed.

"Okay, yeah." Nora set Declan down to give her arms a rest. She'd need her strength if she planned to continue arm wrestling with her father. "I know. We don't have long with Dad. I get it."

She marched back into the room and gritted her teeth. She lasted ninety-two minutes this time, which felt like an eternity. To Declan, too, apparently, as he had upended a tray of medical equipment, turned off the room's lights—twice—and called the nurse's station. The tittering women on the other end of the speaker didn't help. They thought talking to Declan was a riot and encouraged him to keep pushing the button as much as he liked.

Sutton, in a rare act of mercy, managed to fall asleep in the middle of the hubbub.

"I need to…" *Jump off a tall building.* Nora pinched the bridge of her nose. "Use the ladies' room. Be right back."

Eve distracted Declan by opening and closing her mirrored compact, nodding at Nora over her shoulder. "Who's that boy in there? Oh! Where did he go?"

Seeing how Declan instantly loved the game of peek-aboo, Nora decided to veer off in the opposite direction from the ladies' room and instead sought out some much-needed coffee. The lack of sleep the night before had started wearing on her.

But the reason for it—that made it all worthwhile.

Exhaustion must have had her seeing things because she could swear the cause of it had just stepped off the elevator with a stuffed horse the size of Declan under his arm.

Reid's gaze met hers across the corridor. And a slow smile spread across his face.

Her knees went weak. Oh, no. Reid had gotten under her skin when she wasn't looking.

"What are you doing here?" she whispered furiously

as Reid caught up with her in the hall. Weak knees and hospital visits weren't part of the deal. Her resistance was down and there was nothing good that could come of this.

Reid pulled Nora out of the middle of the corridor and into an alcove that afforded them a measure of privacy. "I was concerned about your father."

"Sure you were."

The irony of having recently seen Eve and one of the Newport brothers squashed into a similar alcove wasn't lost on Nora. If anyone who knew her happened by, the speculation would be rampant because this little space was scarcely big enough for one person, let alone two.

Which meant that Reid's arms obviously would fit only if he slipped them around Nora's waist. Since that was where she secretly wanted them, that worked for her, too.

His beautiful face still wore a hint of that amazing ghostly smile, and his wholly masculine scent, much stronger here in closer confines, nearly made her weep.

Somehow, her head tipped up and she landed in the middle of a sweet kiss that seemed to surprise Reid as much as it did her.

He simply held her close as the connection they'd shared last night lit up like an electrical circuit had been completed by the act of joining lips. All the angst and disappointment and hurt from the last few hours at her father's bedside melted away. The difficult morning with a stubborn two-year-old vanished instantly.

And the darkness she sometimes sensed inside Reid—that was gone, too.

This was precisely what she'd needed. *Reid.* Only him. He energized her, enlivened all her nerve endings with a tingle that she couldn't pretend was anything other than the thrill of his presence. Despite all the promises she'd elicited, from him and from herself, he'd come anyway.

It meant something to her. What, she couldn't say yet. Especially since he wasn't supposed to be here. Especially since they were all wrong for each other. Especially since she suddenly couldn't let go of him.

But he didn't deepen the kiss the way she half expected. She appreciated his discretion. They were within sight of her father's hospital room.

When Reid broke off the kiss—far too soon, in her opinion—he nuzzled her ear and she found about a hundred reasons to like that, too.

"No, really," he insisted and his breath warmed her neck. "Sutton is a fixture of Chicago business. Everyone is aware of his health situation and anyone with a pulse would be concerned. I wanted to check on him. And you. See how you were holding up."

"I'm fine."

His brows rose. "Try that on someone who didn't just spend hours learning how to read your subtle nuances, sweetheart. You can give me the real answer."

Something crumbled inside her under the dual spotlights of his brown eyes. "He's a beast, what do you expect? Cancer didn't magically make him into a nice person or a better father."

"Shh." Reid tightened his grip on her and one hand came up to cradle the back of her head as he pressed it to his shoulder.

And that's when she realized she was shaking. Of course he'd misinterpreted that as her needing comfort. But now that she was here, his shoulder was strong and she didn't mind leaning on it. It hid the fact that a couple of tears had worked their way loose and his dark suit jacket absorbed them easily.

"You were gone this morning."

Why had she brought that up? He'd left for really good reasons. None of which she could recall at this moment, but there were some.

"Yeah."

"But you came to the hospital. You don't like being in public."

"No."

His fingers tangled in her hair, stroking across her scalp, comforting her. These one-word responses weren't cutting it. Not when the ground was sliding away at her feet and she couldn't catch it. "You came for me. Why?"

He pulled back enough to capture her jaw with his hands, holding her face up so he could look into her eyes. "You know why. We're not finished. I want to see you, even if it's just for a few more days until you leave. Don't tell me to go."

No way. Her will wasn't that strong. Not with that kind of an admission. So she'd have to push him to leave on his own. "We agreed, Reid. One night. You said it yourself. Where could this possibly lead?"

He blinked and when he opened his eyes, she saw a vulnerability she didn't recognize in their depths. "We did agree. But the problem is, I don't think I can stick to it. I thought we were working through our attraction and that would be that. I've been useless at work for hours. I can't stop thinking about you. Can't we find a way to spend a few days together and *then* answer the question about where this is going to go?"

She was already shaking her head. "Reid, we've been through this. But maybe I wasn't clear enough. I have a son. He has to be at the root of all my decisions. I don't have a few days to play hooky with you while we run around like teenagers having sex in elevators."

"Well, that wasn't what I had in mind at all. But it is now."

She felt the heat rise in her cheeks. "You know what I mean."

"Yeah, but you don't know what I mean."

The corners of his mouth lifted in his ghost of a smile again. But she'd just basically told him to get lost, after he'd pleaded with her not to. Why was he forcing her to be the one making all the hard choices here? It shouldn't be like that.

"It doesn't matter what you meant. I'm a mom. You've got zero interest in kids." Nora had zero interest in finding someone permanent, even if he wanted a dozen kids. "We might as well be from different planets."

"Even if I meant I wanted to spend time with Declan, too?" Reid picked up the stuffed horse, which Nora had forgotten he'd dropped to the floor of the alcove because she was too busy leaning on his strong shoulders. Which she shouldn't have done. It was confusing her.

He was confusing her. "What are you talking about? You want to spend time with me *and* my son?"

Reid nodded as if this was the answer to all their problems. "I'm not trying to turn you into someone who's not a mom. Let me take both of you to Lincoln Park Zoo. They have giraffes. Declan might like to see them."

Oh, no. Declan couldn't be allowed to latch onto Reid as the answer to his "Daadee" quest. After the heartbreaking scene this morning, she couldn't afford to even introduce them to each other. There was no telling what her son would do with it.

"He would like that." What was wrong with her? *Say no. Right now.*

Except Reid's face transformed as he treated her to his rare megawatt smile and she forgot her own name and how to breathe.

The problem was *she* would like to spend more time with Reid, especially after he'd gone to such lengths to ask. Especially after he'd so sweetly included Declan.

Even if it was just for a couple of days, an extension of their one night. She could handle that. Probably.

"Tomorrow, then? We'll make a day of it. I'll take you both to lunch."

She nodded, though she'd have sworn she'd been about to tell him she had plans. *Oh, goodness.* What had she just agreed to?

Nora should have told Reid to take a hike when he'd accosted her at the hospital yesterday. He still didn't understand why she hadn't. It would have saved them both the trouble of ending it later on, because he knew good and well they were living on borrowed time.

No one, least of all Reid, had any illusions about what this was: he was dragging out their one night because he was too selfish to let Nora fade into memory. So selfish that he'd manipulated her into an actual date that included her son.

She should have said no.

Instead, she'd agreed to his impulsive invitation. It was insanity. And felt like the smartest thing he'd ever conceived. The best of both worlds. No one expected him to sign up for Fatherhood Duties and he got to breathe in the scent of vanilla and strawberries while easing the tension and fatigue on Nora's face.

Surreptitiously, he watched Nora as she directed his driver in how to install the car seat the man had carefully placed in the rearmost seat of Reid's limousine. It should look odd, or refuse to fit right. Obviously his driver either had experience at this sort of thing or the gods had blessed this zoo trip—because the seat went in like a charm and Nora got Declan into it with no fuss.

Which was good. Reid wiped his clammy hands on his khaki slacks. Nerves? Really?

But it made a whacked-out sort of sense that foreboding was prickling along the back of his neck. After all, he rarely went out in public. And he'd already tempted the fates by going to the hospital yesterday. Thus far, he'd escaped any sort of media attention, but the odds of that continuing, when he'd be very visible at a huge tourist attraction such as Lincoln Park Zoo, were zilch. The press would work itself into a fever pitch over this and expose Nora to the joys of Chicago's fascination with its "most mysterious bachelor," as well.

He should have thought this through a bit more.

Except then Nora settled in next to him against the creamy leather seat and brushed his thigh with hers. He pushed the negatives to the back of his mind. *What's done is done.* If the media clued in to the fact that he had invited a woman and her son on a date, so be it.

Nora handed Declan a chunky book. He took it immediately and turned it over a couple of times with a little noise of satisfaction. Could the kid read already? Somehow Reid had the impression kids learned to read when they were like five or six. Maybe Declan was one of those Mozart-genius types who would become a prodigy.

Fascinated, Reid watched as Declan stuck the corner

of the book in his mouth. Ah. So he didn't actually *read* it. The book was more of a chew toy. Honestly, Reid would have batted the cardboard out of the kid's mouth with an admonishment that books were for looking at, not eating. Which showed what he knew.

"Thank you," Nora murmured to Reid.

He glanced at her, though he kind of didn't want to miss a minute of observing Nora's son so he could keep demystifying little-boy things. "We haven't even gotten to the zoo yet. Maybe Declan will hate it. You should save your thanks for later."

Nora's warm hazel eyes caught and held his, refusing to let him weasel out of her gratitude. "You gave me an alternative to sitting at the hospital, where I'm forced to watch my father die bit by bit. Anything else will be a great time by comparison, unless the giraffes try to eat us."

Reid couldn't help the smile that flashed over his face. He'd been doing a lot of that lately and couldn't seem to find a reason to stop. "Well, there are some rules on this outing."

She pursed her wide, sexy lips. "Oh, really? Rules like make sure you know where your field trip buddy is at all times?"

As if he needed a rule for that. There was no danger of losing track of her. When she did stuff like that with her mouth, she got his full attention. A Victoria's Secret model could strut by in the tiniest lingerie the company made and he'd never notice.

"Yep. That's the first rule," he replied anyway. He slipped his hand in hers and threaded their fingers together. "So we're going to hold hands the whole time just to be sure we don't lose each other."

Her touch burned his palm, heightening the awareness inside the limo. Reminding him that handholding was the extent of the intimacy available to them when a pint-size audience sat a few feet away. How did people with kids ever find time alone?

"Might be hard to push the stroller if we're holding hands," she informed him pertly. "Can't wait to see how you navigate that."

"I run a billion-dollar hotel conglomerate," he countered. "I can push a stroller and keep up with my field trip buddy at the same time."

He hoped. Actually, he'd forgotten all about the wheeled contraption his driver had loaded into the limo's trunk. But this had been his idea; he'd figure it out.

And somewhere along the way, maybe he'd figure out what he'd hoped to accomplish with this zoo outing. He'd only been trying to take Nash's advice. No one was extending marriage proposals—nor was anyone confused about whether one was forthcoming at some point in the future. It wasn't. Reid and Nora were spending time together without any pressure, without any expectations, until one or both of them decided they were done.

Until then, it gave him a chance to be in her orbit, a place he'd discovered suited him, and also afforded

Reid an opportunity to be around Declan without the white-knuckle panic that had accompanied their first interaction. If this trip to the zoo turned out to be a disaster, then Reid could in good conscience tell Nora it wasn't working out...as Nash had said.

But Reid fully intended to give it the college try, especially if he could somehow find a way to get Declan asleep and contained so he could strip Nora naked later on. The zoo trip had been designed to grease those wheels and he wasn't ashamed to admit it.

"Rule number two is everyone has to have fun," Reid advised her. "So be warned. Anyone who doesn't have fun is banished to the car."

"I'd like to know how you plan to gauge that," she said with a laugh. "Do you have a fun meter in your pocket?"

"Why so many questions?" He squeezed her hand. "You don't trust me?"

Her gaze lit on his and grew heavy with implication. With awareness. With a hundred other things that he should do something to stop. But couldn't.

"I would trust you with my life, Reid. But you'll forgive me if I'm a little skeptical about all of this. Every conversation we've ever had has included your no-kids disclaimer. So yeah, I'm hesitant to embrace the zoo wholeheartedly."

That stung more than Reid would have expected, given that it was true. But it wasn't the whole picture. "I'm...trying something new. Because you're worth it."

Her gaze warmed. "You have no idea what that does to me, do you?"

"What, telling you how special you are?" He shook his head, a little off balance at the direction of the conversation. How had things veered into the realm of significant so quickly? "I hope it makes you ready for fun because that's rule number two, if you recall. Rule number three—"

"You're not changing the subject." She rubbed a thumb over his knuckle in apparent apology for cutting him off. "Humor me. I've been on my own for a long time and then was plunged into my father's health drama. Unwillingly. You're distracting me from both, with style. I appreciate it. This is the second-best date I've ever had."

He wanted to brush it off, to deflect all the *significance* because she had it all wrong. She was the one distracting *him*, treating *him* to an escape from his everyday world where the black swirl of tragedy colored everything. But to say so would only add to the implications, which were already far too deep to ignore.

He shifted uncomfortably but didn't let go of her hand because he liked the feel of it in his. "You're far too easy to impress. Not only has this date not even started yet, I haven't begun to treat you to the date you deserve."

"Well, I can't wait for the follow-up, then. My calendar is suddenly very clear."

"Mine, too," he lied. Or rather it wouldn't be a lie

once he told Mrs. Grant to call everyone he'd ever met and tell them he was busy for the next year.

An overreaction. But warranted. The things Nora made him feel… He never wanted it to end. He was so tired of not feeling. Of being forced to bear his burdens alone. Granted, he'd brought it upon himself, but only because no one else understood. Nor did he want to burden anyone else. Nora blew all of that away.

It would suck when this ended, as it surely would, despite his wishes to the contrary.

Reid's driver pulled up to the entrance of the Lincoln Park Zoo and scurried around to the back to unload Declan's stroller, unfolding it with ease on the sidewalk. Reid waited for Nora to unbuckle the little boy from the car seat and then he helped them both out of the limo. Once Declan was seated, they rolled toward the entrance, Reid pushing the stroller, and he fully appreciated that Nora didn't make one crack about how it actually took two hands to maneuver.

Nine

The third time Declan said, "Jraff," Nora almost burst into tears.

His vocabulary had exploded the last few days. It was miraculous, considering he'd been a slow starter in the speech department. Apparently a trip to the zoo had unleashed the kid's vocal cords.

Reid strolled ahead with Declan, pointing to the black howler monkeys that Nora recalled from trips to the zoo in her youth. Of course, her father had never taken her to the zoo. Not that she was casting Reid in the father role in this scenario. But he was a man and Declan was a child. It wasn't a stretch to think how nice it was to have someone around with strong, masculine arms to push the million-pound stroller that only got heavier as the day wore on.

For goodness' sake, it wasn't just nice. She'd been doing this single-mom thing from day one and it sucked. Only she hadn't realized how hard it had been to be the sole parent until there was someone else around to pick up some of the burden. Was it so bad to wallow in it for a minute?

Reid had already done more with Declan in this one excursion than Sutton had done with Nora in the whole of her life. Her gratefulness knew no bounds. What had started out as reconnecting with an old friend had become something else. Something she hadn't seen coming. *What* that was, she couldn't say. Or rather didn't want to say. Especially when Reid laughed—*laughed*—at something Declan said.

The darkness she'd sensed in Reid from the first moment hadn't returned. It was powerful to think she might have had something to do with that.

She realized he was getting too far ahead of her. How had that happened? This was her day of fun, too, but she'd been too busy soaking in the gorgeous sight of a man pushing her baby in a stroller. The same man who had rescued her from a day of withering away at her father's bedside. Rescued her from the guilt of not trying harder to forgive.

Nora caught up and ignored the flutter in her chest when Reid glanced down at her, his brown eyes full of mirth.

"What's so funny?" she asked.

"Declan would like the monkey to henceforth be named George." Reid ruffled Declan's head as the boy craned his neck to see the people behind him. "He's rather insistent, too."

Nora smiled. "That's the name of the monkey in one of his books. Curious George. Declan can be a bit stubborn when he latches onto something. I have no idea where he gets that from."

They pushed through a knot of people outside the primate house and Reid lit up as he saw the sign for a nearby enclosure. "Zebras. We have to go."

He took off and, breathlessly, she followed. The day was every bit as fun as Reid had commanded it to be but not because she'd done anything special to follow his rules. Reid made it that way. His phone had stayed in his pocket except for a brief thirty seconds at the tail end of lunch when he scrolled through it, but then it disappeared again. Up until that point, she hadn't even realized he'd brought it.

His sole focus had been on Declan. Surprisingly. She'd half thought he'd invented this zoo trip as a way to butter her up so she'd say yes when he tried to charm his way into her bed again. If so, she would have been happy to tip him off that no zoo was required for that. Their whole relationship centered on what happened in the bedroom…and sometimes the living room. But that didn't change facts. They were sleeping together but that was it. All she'd let it be.

Which made this whole excursion that much more mystifying.

When they finally fell into the limo, exhausted and happy at the end of a long day, Reid captured her hand again and held it tight. "Navy Pier. Tomorrow. Don't make me beg."

"What?" She stared at him, trying to make the words fit the agenda she'd swear he had, but couldn't figure out. "You want to take us to an amusement park? Tomorrow? You have work."

I have another long day at the hospital. All at once, she didn't want to go back there, not on the heels of the alternative Reid had supplied her with.

"I do not have work. Oh, I mean, I do. The hotel industry doesn't sleep, no pun intended." He flashed that gorgeous smile he seemed to pass out rather freely now, and yet it still affected her exactly as it had in the hospital corridor yesterday—as if she'd been hit in the solar plexus by a freight train. "But I don't have anything that can't wait," he continued. "You're leaving soon. I'll catch up later."

Guilt coated the back of Nora's throat. She definitely wasn't staying in Chicago. Nothing could convince her to come back to this hellhole permanently, not even the death of the man who'd made it so miserable for her. But as she'd been using her imminent departure as an excuse to push away any hint of this thing between her and Reid blossoming into something more, she should correct his assumptions.

"My schedule is pretty open-ended. I wasn't sure what was happening with Dad, so I didn't buy a return plane ticket in case…well, I ended up having to help organize a funeral." Quickly, she rushed on. "So there's no hammer going down anytime soon. You certainly don't have to take off work to entertain us."

"Nora." Reid tipped up her chin so she met his gaze squarely. "I'm not entertaining you, like you need a tour guide for the city you grew up in. Don't be so silly. I'm spending time with you and Declan because I want to."

Oh. His sincerity convinced her and since there was nothing she wanted to do less than sit at the hospital, she found herself nodding. "Then we'd love it. Right, Declan?"

He nodded drowsily, his forehead resting against the padded car seat lip. He fell asleep on the way back to her father's guesthouse and in another surprising move, Reid insisted on carrying the sleeping toddler into his room, placing him gently on the crib mattress with ease.

"You'd think you'd done that a million times," Nora said with a laugh as soon as Reid shut the door to Declan's room.

"I might have googled it," he admitted with a chagrined expression. "I guess some people are born with the parenting gene, but I have to depend on technology to figure out how to get a kid into a crib."

"No one is born with the parenting gene. We all have to struggle through it and figure things out." Her heart tightened, wringing out some emotions she'd have sworn were dead and buried.

He'd done research on how to put a baby to bed? Reid didn't want to have anything to do with kids. Why, in all that was holy, would he have done that—unless he'd planned to be in a position to need the information? Something had changed fundamentally and she scrambled to wrap her mind around it.

"And now for my follow-up," he murmured and swept Nora up in his arms, Rhett Butler–style.

Breathless, Nora clung to his neck, but that was strictly to steady herself. There was no danger of Reid dropping her as he carried her to her bedroom without one hitch in his stride. He kicked the door behind them and placed her on the bedspread. The sudden heat in his gaze left no room for misinterpreting what he'd meant by "follow-up."

"Did you google 'getting a mom into bed,' too?" she asked with raised eyebrows, her hands fisting against the bed in search of something to hold on to as the look in his eye told her she was in for a wild ride.

"That's one I didn't have to research."

In a flash, he stripped off his khaki pants and button-down shirt, treating her to the best sight of the day—Reid in all his naked splendor. She sucked in a breath as everything went liquid inside.

Just as quickly, he got her out of her clothes and rolled her into his arms, murmuring against her neck. They'd had some pretty inventive sex thus far, and Nora geared herself up for something that could rightly be called a "follow-up."

But in another surprise after a long day of them, Reid seemed intent on something different still: slow, languorous lovemaking.

She fell into the sensations, savoring them as he kissed her long and deep, touched her everywhere with a kind of reverence. When he finally pushed into her with a maddeningly unhurried glide that threatened to drive her off the edge, the perfection of it squeezed a tear loose from her.

A *tear*. It was only sex, for crying out loud. But when she focused on Reid as he withdrew, then repeated his torturous reentry, he caught her gaze. That smile spilled over his face, transforming him from the inside out.

Transforming *her*. This wasn't old friends becoming something more. It was a spiritual joining of two people, and she couldn't hold back any longer. Her heart exploded with so many unnameable things at the same moment as her body did. Things she needed to shut down—*immediately*. But couldn't. She was lost to this man.

Reid tensed with a low groan, experiencing his own release on the heels of hers, then gathered her close as if he'd never let go.

But he had to. Eventually. Nothing lasted forever and Nora was tired of losing things. It was better to never grab onto them in the first place.

* * *

Reid knocked on the door of the Winchester guest-house for the third time in three days.

It was a habit he'd been trying to think of a reason to break and had failed miserably. He liked Nora. She always had a quick smile, her wry sense of humor matched his and she'd learned exactly how to use that wide mouth to drive him to the brink.

Sometimes, he let her push him over the edge because it was just that amazing when she took it upon herself to pleasure him. He always made it up to her later, though, usually twice. If he played his cards right, hopefully that would be on the agenda later tonight after they made an appearance at this pesky Foundation for Education fundraiser he'd agreed to attend.

Since he was on the board—because doing charitable works for kids should assuage his guilt over his niece and nephew, and yet, did not—he felt obligated to go. And for some reason he'd yet to fathom, Nora had agreed to be his plus-one. She shouldn't have. A public appearance together at a black-tie event was sure to get the tongues of Chicago wagging. But he could imagine only Nora at his side. Which had also become a bit of a habit that he couldn't figure out how to break.

When Nora swung open the door, Reid nearly forgot how to breathe.

"Wow." That was all that he could squeeze out around the sudden lump in his throat.

"It's okay?" she asked.

She spun around, sending the floor-length skirt of her dress flowing. It was the color of deep sapphire, strapless, with little folds of fabric over her breasts that highlighted one of her best features. She'd put her hair up in a loose bun, leaving tendrils to fall around her face. A glittery collar of blue stones that matched her dress circled her throat, winking in the low light of the setting sun.

But that sparkle paled in comparison with the woman.

"No," he murmured, not quite trusting his voice. "It's the opposite of okay unless you want to skip this black-tie shindig and go lock ourselves in your bedroom for a few hours. If that was your goal—bingo."

She laughed and waved over her shoulder at her sister Grace, who was just visible beyond the foyer playing with Declan on his patchwork quilt. "We're off. Back by ten."

"As if," Grace called. "I brought an overnight bag. Don't even bother acting like you didn't see it. I'm here till morning. Don't waste the opportunity."

Well, then. Grace might have just moved into the number one spot as Reid's favorite relative of Nora's. Or maybe she shared that spot with Declan. Imagine Reid's surprise as he'd developed a fondness for the kid over the last few days.

Of course the boy still scared the bejesus out of him with his fragile little body and inability to communicate in something other than short words and phrases that were impossible to decipher. Reid spent half his time in Declan's presence making sure he didn't do something wrong, which was stressful and frustrating. But the other half of the time, the kid was amazing. Funny, inquisitive, fearless.

Nora shut the door and it was just the two of them on the front steps. Reid swallowed as the reality hit him. This wasn't an excursion to the zoo or to Navy Pier that he could blow off as spending time with an old friend and her son if anyone questioned him. Or that he could justify to himself as nothing special. This was a real date in public with Nora Winchester O'Malley on his arm. The paparazzi would be there in full force as the whole point of the fundraiser was to get publicity for the foundation. There was nowhere to hide. No excuses.

He was dating Nora. And vice versa.

Maybe going public wouldn't be as invasive as he was envisioning.

That hope smashed into little pieces as the limo snaked toward the entrance of the Field Museum. The number of people in the throng of onlookers, most armed with cameras sporting telephoto lenses, was truly frightening.

"Sure you're ready for this?" he asked Nora.

"Not really, no," she admitted. "I practiced my dance steps all day but I'm relatively hopeless. I'm probably not going to enhance your reputation any."

"Ha. That's a lie. You enhance my reputation just

by being on my arm," he shot back. "And I was talking about being ready for a public splash."

He hated the idea of their privacy being invaded, their lives raked over by strangers who had never spoken two words to either of them. There would be photos flung across the internet far and wide with ridiculous captions like Reclusive Billionaire Corrupts Chicago Real Estate Mogul's Daughter.

So far, they'd managed to avoid attention but that wouldn't last forever. In fact, judging by the frenzy of the crowd as his driver pulled to the curb, parked and came around to let them out, they'd just become very visible in the public eye.

"Oh. Yeah, I'm sorry, but you're the one who's mainly affected by that. I'll go home and no one will even remember my name." She waved it off. "That was part of the draw in vacating Chicago, after all. I also removed myself from the limelight. The socialite scene wears on you. I don't miss it."

What would it be like to just walk away? That was a scenario he'd never considered—but should have. All at once, it sounded heavenly. What better way to avoid all the gossip and speculation and people he didn't want to be around than to go somewhere else?

Of course, he couldn't run his empire unless he was in the middle of it. Other people might be able to handle working remotely, but not Reid. He breathed his hotels like air and liked it.

But the idea of chucking it all stuck with him as he

helped Nora from the limo and hooked her hand on his arm to tread the red carpet lining the roped-off area leading to the entrance. Flashes bathed them as a hundred photographs were snapped in under a minute. Reid was grateful when they finally made it inside the museum. All the street noise was cut off instantly.

Faint strains of Mozart piped through the great hall from hidden speakers. Two dozen tables with white cloths and tea lights had been strewn about the cavernous space; one corner housed an elephant statue and a grand piano. A couple hundred of Chicago's elite worked the room, wheeling and dealing. More money would change hands under this roof than on the whole Magnificent Mile the weekend before Christmas.

"Eve's here somewhere," Nora commented as she craned her neck to scan the crowds. "She made me promise to say hi so she could see how the dress turned out. She had it sent over."

"There she is." Reid nodded as he spied Nora's willowy sister. "Dancing with Graham Newport."

Very cozily, as a matter of fact. The dance floor had been set up a good hundred yards from the entrance, but even at that distance, Reid could see the possessive slant to Newport's hold on Eve Winchester. Surprising, given the drama going on with the Winchester fortune, that Eve would fraternize with a Newport, but she didn't seem terribly put off by the proximity of her dance partner. They were so close, you couldn't wedge a sheet of paper between them.

It looked as if Nora wasn't the only Winchester sister making a public confession about her love life this evening.

"Huh." Nora zeroed in on her sister, a speculative look in her eye. "There's something going on there, which she has thus far refused to admit to. She's being very cagey about it, but there's no way she can shrug it off now."

"Especially not if we go dance near them." Which suited Reid's purposes as well, since he had a strong need to get Nora into his arms. The scent of vanilla and strawberries was particularly alluring this evening and it had been driving him nuts since the moment they got into the limo. "Assuming you want to dance?"

Nora's wide smile answered that question.

"Sure that's Graham?" she asked as Reid took her hand to lead her to the dance floor. "I don't know the twins well enough to tell them apart."

"I do," Reid said curtly, without explanation.

He'd crossed paths with the brothers more than once; they got around. That one was Graham for sure. He had a reserved demeanor about him you couldn't miss, a wait-and-see approach that was the opposite of his brother's. Brooks had a hot head and a quick mouth that sometimes got him into trouble as he leaped without looking more often than not.

Which made it all the more perplexing that Graham was the one making time with a Winchester sister. If there was some nefarious intent behind their interaction, Reid would have put money on Brooks being involved.

Then everything else slid away as he swept Nora into his arms and held her close.

"This is the first time we've danced," he murmured. "I like it."

"Me, too." She peered up through those matchless hazel eyes, which had gone a bit soft and warm, and everything good in the world was right here. In his grasp.

Not for the first time, his gut knotted. She would leave soon. He did *not* like that. This thing between them wasn't burning itself out and he was in a bit of a quandary over the next steps. Mostly because he didn't see any miracles popping up that would fix all the roadblocks between them.

Neither of them had any business thinking of next steps.

He was going to have to say goodbye. Soon. He flat out didn't know how he was going to do it. Usually, that was the easiest word in the English language to utter. It should have been the easiest here, too, especially given Nora's permanent plus-one.

But goodbye wasn't happening tonight. Grace had given them a pass on what time they returned, which didn't even have to be until morning. Reid intended to take full advantage of it.

Eve and Graham finally noticed Reid and Nora dancing near them, though how they'd yanked their attention away from each other was beyond him. The couple sprang apart as if they'd been caught spray painting graffiti on the Cloud Gate sculpture in Millennium Park.

"Oh, hey, Nora," Eve called and crossed her arms, then uncrossed them to let them dangle at her sides. "I didn't know you'd arrived yet."

"Yeah, you seemed pretty busy." Nora nodded at her sister's dance partner. "Hi, Graham. Nice to see you again, especially outside of the hospital."

There was a hint of frost in Nora's voice that Reid didn't recognize. He was glad it wasn't directed at him as her warmth was one of the things he craved in the middle of the night, when he woke up, alone and freezing, after a particularly vivid nightmare about Sophia and his mom.

Eve blushed, which seemed out of place on a no-nonsense, confident woman. Even as a kid, she'd been authoritative and decisive, with a take-no-prisoners approach. He'd always admired that.

Another couple nearly collided with the now-stationary group in the center of the dance floor.

"Well, I'm headed to the bar," Eve said brightly. "Thanks for the dance, Graham."

Reid nodded to Eve and Newport as they edged away, clearly uncomfortable with the audience. But as Reid was still dancing with Nora and loath to stop, he didn't worry about the dynamics of whatever was going on with Eve and Newport.

He just wanted to soak up as much Nora as he could

and worry later about the screeching halt to their relationship, which loomed on the horizon.

At dinner, he and Nora predictably ended up at a table with Eve and Graham, as well as Brooks and his date, a bombshell model from Hungary who spoke little English. Brooks and Graham scarcely noticed her lack of conversation once they got going on what appeared to be a hot topic—their opinions about Nora's father, his money and the half brother they shared with the Winchester sisters.

The rib eye and lobster weren't bad, so Reid ate his dinner and stayed out of it until Brooks mentioned that he'd called an old friend who was a lawyer to help with his case against Sutton.

Nora flushed and laid down her fork. "You called a lawyer to fight my father? What on earth for?"

"Because Winchester's up to something. When the paternity test came back negative for us, he admitted he wasn't our father but then clammed up. He knows who our father is. I need him to spill his guts," Brooks explained. "And Carson has a stake in ironing out details, too, since he's an heir. An impartial lawyer can only help both situations. We can't be too careful."

"Carson is not an 'heir,'" Eve insisted with exaggerated air quotes and a hearty scowl. "He's nowhere in Dad's will and Winchester blood doesn't automatically earn Carson the right to anything."

Nora's mouth turned down and it was clear the conversation was upsetting her. Reid squeezed her hand under the table as everyone else forgot about eating in favor of jumping into the argument full steam.

"We say differently," Graham retorted. "Our friend Josh Calhoun is stopping by here on his way home to Iowa. He's a legal expert who should be able to shed some insight and then we'll see what's what. You can't block us from getting what's rightfully ours."

"What about what's rightfully *ours*?" Eve glowered at the man she'd just been dancing with so cozily. "Carson didn't have the pleasure of growing up as a Winchester. Our dad's estate belongs to those of us who suffered for years at his hands."

Brooks nearly came out of his seat. "You don't think Carson's suffered over Winchester's selfishness? That SOB knew he'd fathered a kid and never bothered to claim him."

"He's lucky," Eve shot back. "Some days, I wish I'd never been claimed. But trust me when I tell you that the billions Carson thinks he's due belong to me, Grace and Nora. Period."

"Stop it!" Nora pushed back from the table and stood as the other diners at nearby tables began to murmur about the drama. "Fighting like this doesn't solve anything. We can't stop you from getting additional legal help, so you boys do what you think you need to do. But leave me out of it. It's only money and I don't want any of it."

With that, Nora spun and fled the hall. Reid nodded to the other stunned guests and followed her. He found her in the lobby, huddled in a corner. When he gathered her up in his arms, his stomach clenched as the tears running down her cheeks caught the light.

But then she clung to him and gave a soft little sigh that thrummed through him, winnowing under his skin, making everything better just because they were together. A dangerous fullness in his chest spread and it felt so good, he couldn't find a reason to stop it.

"I hate to ask, but would you mind if we left?" Her voice was muffled against his shoulder. "I know my family is ruining your party, but—"

"No one's ruining anything," he broke in. "If you want to leave, we're leaving."

He was the last person to argue with the idea of getting the hell out of Dodge, especially when the flip side meant that he got to have Nora all to himself. This surely wasn't his scene and if anyone didn't like that he'd left early, they could make an appointment during business hours for some time in the next century to complain about it.

"Thanks." She took a deep, shuddery breath and flashed a watery smile. "You've developed a habit of rescuing me from bad situations. I've kind of grown fond of it."

"I'm happy to be your knight in shining armor," he said gruffly, as the gratitude radiating from her eyes added to the already heavy moment. There were things going on here that couldn't be ignored. But they were not things he felt equipped to deal with.

Because at the end of the day, anything other than saying goodbye could only be described as selfish, selfish and even more selfish.

But as the night was still young and he'd never claimed to be a saint, he took full advantage of Grace's pass and ferried Nora back to his penthouse. They made love in his bed, and he surprised himself by asking Nora if she'd stay. Which he desperately wanted all at once. He'd been breaking all his rules left and right. What was one more? Especially when he felt the end of their relationship snapping at his heels like a rabid dog.

But she shook her head. "I've never slept apart from Declan. I'm sure I'll have to eventually but I'm not rushing it."

Reid let her go through an act of sheer will. He slept alone in his bed after all, his rules still intact, but not by his own choice.

But the morning news brought a healthy reminder of the situation.

Front and center in his newsfeed was a photograph of Nora on his arm as they exited his limo. But the caption didn't include the usual sexual innuendo, or allude to his playboy reputation and his status as a recluse. Instead, it asked a question that shocked him to the core: Is Chicago's Most Eligible Bachelor off the Market?

Had everyone clued in that he was falling for Nora before he had?

Ten

The days after the fundraiser dragged miserably. Nora didn't hear from Reid other than a slew of funny text messages at odd hours. While she appreciated that Reid was clearly thinking about her as much as she was thinking about him, she felt his absence keenly. More than she would have anticipated.

Declan played his game of searching for "Daadee" at least once a day and it killed her every time. She found herself daydreaming of a life free of complications, heartbreak and terminal diagnoses. Of course Reid had to get back to work and she had to get back to the reason she'd come to Chicago, though.

She'd done her duty by her father and gone to the hospital every day, even though it meant wading through hordes of media mongers who had begun following her constantly. Apparently, the scandal regarding Carson's parentage coupled with the photograph of Nora on Reid's arm at the fundraiser had thrust her back into the limelight, the last place she wanted to be, the place she'd fled to Colorado to escape.

"I'm going to get some coffee," she announced to Sutton's personal assistant after a particularly long afternoon when her father had been awake more than usual.

It wore on her to listen to the endless lectures about how she should be raising Declan and her father's imperious demands that she move back to Chicago and "act like a Winchester."

Her counterargument—that she was an O'Malley and therefore not subject to patriarchal tyranny—hadn't gone over well.

Valerie nodded to acknowledge Nora's announcement. "Eve's been in the lounge for an hour. You might want to check on her to see if she's okay."

"Sure."

Nora sighed as she punched in the code for the family lounge area and pushed open the door. The smell of freshly brewed coffee nearly made her weep. She'd been dragging lately, sleeping fitfully and waking in a bleary-eyed stupor. It wasn't like her and she'd chalk it up to being back in Chicago to anyone who asked. But she had a feeling it was deeper than that and had

Reid's name written all over it, which she did *not* want to examine.

The feelings she'd been ignoring seemed like a betrayal of Sean, and she wasn't dealing with that well. Nor did ignoring them make them go away.

Eve sat in a wingback chair near the window, staring out at the hospital parking lot as she nursed her own cup of coffee.

"On the lookout for loverboy?" Nora said by way of greeting.

Eve's head whipped around and the scowl on her face could have peeled the paint off the walls. "What's that supposed to mean?"

"Wow. I should call Grace and tell her she lucked out in volunteering to stay with Declan at the house instead of subjecting herself to the bad moods around here. But then, if she's drinking the same Kool-Aid, I'll just get my head bitten off."

"Maybe you should look in the mirror for the reason people are particularly touchy today," Eve advised her with a smirk. "You're rubbing everyone the wrong way. What's the matter? Reid finally stop calling? It was bound to happen. Women bounce off him like he's a trampoline. No one gets his attention for long."

"Hey. Leave Reid out of this." Was that what had happened? Their relationship had run its course? Sadness crowded into her chest all at once. She'd kind of thought they'd have a few more days together at least.

Somehow, the fact that Eve had clued in on it before

Nora had made it worse. Her sister had obviously seen Reid's dating habits up close and personal since they ran into each other at least a few times a year. But it didn't matter. Nothing had happened that Nora hadn't already been preparing herself for. Things were going to end eventually. Why not now?

"Besides, it's not like that," Nora said a little more forcefully. "We're just old friends. Nothing more."

"Sure. That's why you're in a crabby mood."

"I'm not in a crabby mood! You're the one who's being weird about your love life."

Eve flinched and then tried to cover it by nonchalantly sipping her coffee. "I don't know what you mean."

Nora latched onto her sister's deflection with a bit of desperation. "Want me to spell it out? G-R-A-H—"

"There's nothing going on between me and Graham Newport," Eve shot back furiously, but not before Nora noted a heaping ton of guilt in her gaze. "I danced with him one time at a stupid fundraiser. Sue me. I'm not the one whose photograph is burning up the gossip sites as we speak."

Nora laughed but it sounded forced. Because it was. "That's old news. You're mistaken if you think anyone cares about a photograph of me and Reid."

Silently, Eve picked up her phone, tapped it a few times and scrolled through the plethora of hits on Nora's name, some as recent as a few moments ago. *Ridiculous.*

Nora's pulse jumped into her throat as she read page after page of perfect strangers commenting on her love life, including theories on whether she was into kinky sex or just put up with it for a shot at landing someone as mysterious and reclusive as Reid. There were also guesses as to whether Nora might next appear with an engagement ring on her finger.

She shook her head. "People need something better to do with their lives than speculate on something as inane as whether Reid is off the market. Besides, as you just pointed out, he's probably already forgotten about me. There isn't much to gossip about."

Nora crossed to get that much-needed cup of coffee and was shocked to see her hands were shaking.

If Reid did find some time in his schedule to see her again, she'd say no. She had to. She had no desire to expose Declan to this level of scrutiny, and that was surely next if the media chose to pick up on her status as a single mom. They'd have a field day with captions about whether Reid had hung up his handcuffs in favor of a baby carriage.

Actually, she'd be hard-pressed to say which idea was more ludicrous—Reid's reputation as a man with unusual tastes, or Reid as a father.

When her phone beeped, she almost didn't pull it from her pocket. She wasn't in the mood for another random text message from Reid with a noncommittal joke about chickens crossing the road.

But that wasn't the message.

I'm downstairs. I need to see you.

Yes. She needed that, too. So desperately. Thank goodness he was here. Her fingers flew to respond: Where?

In my car. Come down? I don't want to give anyone a chance to photograph us.

Brilliant, brilliant man. A smile spread across her face before she could catch it and then she was half-way out the door before she remembered to tell Eve to go back to their father's room. "I've got to go. Can you go sit with Dad?"

Nora shut the door on her sister's groan and high-tailed it to the elevator. Once the doors slid closed, common sense wormed its way to the forefront. This wasn't a chance to get hot and heavy in his limo, though that was probably exactly what was on his mind. And hers.

Dang it. She'd have to take the high road and inform him it was over. They couldn't keep doing this. Disappointment settled low in her belly, but once again, she had to take control of the situation before it got out of hand. She still had the final word about what went on in her life.

When she got outside, she dived into the limo, head down and face shielded from the lenses of the paparazzi who seemed like a permanent fixture at the entrance to Midwest Regional these days. The moment the door closed, Reid swept her into his arms before she could squeak out a protest. And then her brain drained out the moment his lips touched hers.

Oh, yes. She'd missed him, missed his taste, missed his hands in her hair. And she couldn't pull away. She just needed one more second. Which turned into two and then three…and his hands drifted to her waist, where his clever fingers sought her bare skin.

Through some force of will, she surfaced and slapped a palm on his chest to push him back.

"Wait," she commanded breathlessly even as she curled her fingers into the soft cloth of his shirt, almost dragging him back to finish what he'd started. "I have a few things to say before my clothes end up on the other seat."

Reid smirked. "You're going to do a striptease? All right, if you insist. Carry on."

She bit back a laugh. How did he make her laugh so easily as she was about to embark on a difficult conversation? "I meant before *you* start taking them off. We have to talk."

"I know." He threw up a hand, a chagrined expression on his face. "I'm sorry I've been incommunicado but I had some things I needed to handle. I should have called."

She waved it off as if it was no big deal and all was forgiven. Really, that should be the case. The disappointment and heartsick moments at 3:00 a.m. were her fault, not his. "It's fine. It was a good breaking point for us anyway. The gossipmongers have been out in full force, as I'm sure you're aware. That's what I wanted to discuss. We shouldn't see each other anymore."

"I thought so, too," he admitted. "I tried to stay away. I really did. It didn't work for me."

Oh, it *so* hadn't worked for her, either. But that wasn't the point. "Well, we'll have to try harder. Between the media breathing down my neck and my dad—"

All at once, the horrific day came crashing down on her and broke her voice into pieces.

Instantly, Reid gathered her up in his strong arms and she let him because…well, there was really no excuse except she needed someone to care and he did. It was in his touch, in the soft words he murmured into her hair. The tears she'd been fighting didn't seem so weak after all. A few squeezed out, falling onto his gorgeous suit.

She was crying all over Reid Chamberlain and he wasn't pulling away. The way he should. *Good.* She was so tired of being an adult. She'd done about all the adult stuff she could handle for the day. His fingers slid across the back of her neck, cradling her against him, and it was the most peace she'd felt in days.

"What happened with your father?" he asked and the concern in his tone nearly undid her.

If nothing else, Reid was her friend and she had precious few of those. "The usual Sutton Winchester stuff. I guess I'm just particularly affected by it today."

"Because I haven't been around," he finished for her and guilt laced his flat statement. "You can say it. I left you high and dry and didn't call. But I'm here now. Let me take care of you."

With a really spectacular orgasm? She didn't know

whether to laugh or cry some more. Mostly because it sounded like the best plan she'd ever heard in her life. "That's not your job, though I appreciate the sentiment. I've been taking care of myself for a really long time."

He pulled back and pierced her with his brown eyes, which were still swimming with concern. But he didn't let go of her and she started to wonder if he ever would.

"You need to get away from all of this. I'm not kidding. You're letting your father get to you. You don't owe him anything and this bedside vigil is killing you. Why are you still here catering to your family's demand that you come back to Chicago?"

"Because—" All at once, she didn't have an answer. Why *was* she still here? Certainly not for her father, who wasn't going to turn into someone new so she could magically forgive him, as Reid had just painfully helped her remember. Oh, goodness. Had she been waiting for Reid to come around? "Because..."

Gently, he smiled. "Why don't you go home?"

Home. The word permeated her mind. Yes, that's where she wanted to go. "I can't go home. My dad is dying. My family—"

"Will be fine. You said he has until New Year's. That's months away. It's not like sticking around is going to cure his cancer, Nora." His fingers caressed her neck, warming her, and she was a little ashamed she leaned into his touch. "You said you didn't have a return plane ticket. Let me take you home. I have a private jet that's just sitting around."

She swallowed the *yes*. Now was not the time to crumble under the premise that Reid was—once again—rescuing her from her life. The fantasy world he'd drawn her into needed to be over. "That's not necessary. I can fly commercial."

"But you don't have to. Let me take care of you," he insisted. "I want to. Let me. If not for you, then for Declan."

She hadn't seen that trump card coming. Her will melted away as if she'd left it in the rain. The lovely thought of not having to fly in a crowded plane with a two-year-old grabbed onto her and wouldn't let go.

She could go home, get away from the media's fixation on her relationship with Reid, remove Declan from the reach of their sharp claws—and avoid the hospital, where nothing in the form of reconciliation seemed to be happening.

How could she pass up what was simply an act of kindness from an old friend?

"What if my dad needs me?" Even she heard the feebleness in that argument, and Reid didn't let her get away with it.

He snorted. "Sutton needs a swift kick in the rear. And that's all I'll say about that. If anyone needs you, they know how to use the phone. Get away for a while and then come back, if that's your concern."

"You make it sound so easy." She smiled to take away the sting. "Some of us don't have access to a private plane to jet around whenever the whim strikes us."

"Then I'll stay until you're ready to come back," he replied nonchalantly.

"What do you mean, stay? As in *stay*? In Colorado?" Her voice had just entered the decibel range where only dogs could hear her, but *really*? "Reid, that's crazy."

And exactly what she wanted. Oh, yes, she did. Crazy, wonderful togetherness. Not an empty bed and even emptier heart.

"No crazier than trying to live my life here in Chicago with the media firestorm going on. I hate that you're affected by it, too. Besides, I told you. Staying away wasn't working for me. This affords us an opportunity to spend time together without all these eyes on us. So we're solving all our problems at once."

"But we're not… That is, you and I—" She couldn't even put a label on what she and Reid were. How did they get to a place where they were talking about continuing their relationship instead of ending it? A place where she *wanted* to talk about it?

"Stop thinking so hard, Nora." Without taking his eyes off her, he took her hand in his and held it to his lips. "Escape with me. Just for a little while. Let's be crazy and indulgent and ignore the outside world. Fall into the moment. Neither of us do that enough."

The beauty of his suggestion wrapped itself around her like a web, ensnaring her firmly. Real life had beaten her down so much that she'd forgotten how to seize the moment. Reid understood that and was offering her a chance to learn again.

Do not say yes. Do not say yes. But then…why shouldn't she?

He wasn't proposing. He wasn't saying he was staying forever. It was an extension of their wild, wonderful affair far away from those who were trying to turn it into something else. She could put off saying goodbye to the man who had become far more important than he should have.

"Okay. Take me home."

She'd have to deal with saying goodbye soon. But not today. And hopefully the fallout wouldn't include any broken hearts. Well, she'd just make sure of it.

When Reid woke, the smell of vanilla and strawberries clued him in that the cocoon he'd fallen into while in Colorado hadn't vanished while he slept.

His eyes blinked open and sure enough, Nora lay firmly encased in his arms, exactly where she'd been last night. Naked, lush, beautiful. He couldn't recall the last time he'd slept with a woman until morning. He liked it.

Kissing her awake had become as necessary as breathing and he didn't hesitate to indulge. That's what this little foray into craziness was about after all. Doing what felt right. Ignoring the voices in his head that said he was letting this woman hook him far deeper than he had any right to allow.

As he turned her head to take her mouth, she responded instantly, her body coming alive against his, sensation rushing along his skin as her backside drew flush with his raging erection. His hands flew to her breasts. He was desperate to touch, desperate to enflame her in kind.

She tilted her hips backward, adjusting herself against him. Groaning with the effort to stop from sliding right into her, as he ached to do, he half rolled over to blindly fumble for the condoms he'd hidden in her dresser the moment they'd arrived yesterday.

Finally, finally, he sank into the heaven of Nora's body. She took him deep and then deeper still as they moved in tandem, driving each other to the peak of bliss and back down the other side. The release was so much more than physical. He had no way to describe the way she filled him so there was no room for the misery that had lived inside him for so long.

How he'd convinced her to let him follow her to her home in Silver Falls, Colorado, he'd never know. All he knew was that he couldn't stand being away from her. He wanted to explore these new feelings for her that were so big and so important he could barely articulate them. So he'd shot for the stars and had been richly rewarded. So far.

They'd only just started down this seize-the-moment path and he liked not knowing what came next.

Eventually, they rolled from bed and got dressed, then saw to breakfast, which they ate sitting around the distressed pine table in Nora's kitchen. Her whole house was quaint, with a farmhouse style that absolutely fit her. He just hated that she was living here alone, without the benefit of her father's money to make her life easier.

Good thing he was here and could fill in the gaps.

As Reid finished his coffee and scrolled through the morning's headlines on his iPad, Nora ate cereal and chatted. Declan sat in his high chair, his gaze fastened firmly on Reid as if evaluating this new element in his environment. Once he focused his attention on the breakfast his mom had given him, she stood and announced she had about a million loads of laundry.

It was all very domestic. He liked that, too. He'd never had anything like this experience, which suddenly felt like a shame. There'd been a huge hole in his life that he'd only just discovered.

"Need some help?" he asked.

She snickered. "Do you even know what a washing machine looks like?"

"Sure, I've seen them lots of times," he returned easily. "In TV commercials. How hard can it be?"

"It would be a much bigger help if you sat here with Declan and made sure that he doesn't tip his high chair over." Nora tugged on one of Declan's red curls affectionately. "He's becoming quite the climber, aren't you, Butterbean?"

"Bean," Declan echoed and shoved a few more dry cheerios in his mouth.

"You can get him down when he's finished eating, right?" Nora called over her shoulder as she headed toward the bedrooms.

Reid and Declan eyed each other. "It's you and me, sport."

Declan nodded. "Daadee."

Reid blinked. "Uh…"

Clearly, this was not one of those times when the kid lacked communication skills. How had he never realized that Declan might draw some conclusions about Reid's presence in his life and interpret all of this in his own way?

"No, I'm not your dad. Though he was a great man. He fought for our freedom in a very dark place and wasn't able to come home."

For some reason, that choked Reid up. It was a raw deal for Nora and her son, but she'd handled the challenges of becoming a widow with grace. She'd created an amazing house that was every inch a home, with crayon scribbles posted on the refrigerator and toys strewn around the living room.

Despite the darkness of her circumstances, she hadn't let it affect her. It was amazing. He wanted to learn from her example.

"Daadee," Declan repeated, and pointed at Reid.

Reid shook his head. "No, bud. Just because we hung out that night doesn't mean I can do it again. I'm really good at telling other people what to do but they're adults and paid to listen. I—"

He broke off because it wasn't as if Declan could understand how difficult this whole subject was for Reid.

Especially when he didn't understand it himself. He

stared at the redheaded pint-size human in the high chair less than two feet from Reid's chair. The kid had wormed his way into Reid's limited circle of people he cared about, and that made all of this worse. Declan and Nora needed someone with far more to offer than a brooding loner who was marking the days until he could return to his lair and shut himself away from the world again.

Except the concept didn't seem as appealing as it had in the past.

Reid's penthouse didn't have the same feel as Nora's house. His style leaned toward sharp, modern, stark. He would have insisted that he preferred it right up until the time he walked through Nora's door and felt the difference between the two.

At Nora's house, her warmth emanated from the very walls. He wanted to soak it up as long as possible. As long as she'd let him. There was nothing in his penthouse or his work at Chamberlain Group that could compare with having a lover and a friend rolled into one. As Nora had often said, money didn't buy happiness and he got that in a way he never had before.

Nora bustled back into the kitchen. "First load is in the machine and it's not even nine o'clock. That's a personal record."

Her sunny smile felt like a reward that he eagerly accepted.

Nora's phone beeped and they both glanced at it

where it lay on the long island that separated the kitchen from the dining area. She frowned. "It's Eve."

She picked up the phone and thumbed up the message, then shook her head and made a little noise of disgust. "She says my dad wants to talk to me and would I please Skype her. That's just like him. It's not like he can pick up the phone himself. He's got to make it as difficult as possible on everyone else."

"So don't do it," Reid advised and Declan threw a Cheerio on the floor as his vote in the matter.

"Then he'll just take it out on Eve and Grace. That's how he operates." Her mouth tightened. "Better to get it over with, which I honestly think is part of his strategy."

She retrieved her small, off-brand laptop from the built-in desk near the kitchen and set it on the table to boot it up. Eve answered a few seconds after Nora clicked Call, and her sister appeared in the chat window.

"Thanks, Nora. Here's Dad." Eve shifted her own laptop to aim the video lens toward Sutton.

Sutton Winchester's gaunt face filled the screen. *Wow.* Reid had known the man was sick. Dying. But his appearance had so degenerated, it was a bit of a shock. He was pretty sure her father couldn't see him sitting near Nora because of the angle of her laptop, but Nora could, so he kept his alarm to himself. She knew her father didn't have long. She didn't need Reid to add to her burden.

"Nora." Sutton's imperious voice rang out in the

small breakfast nook. "I'm very disappointed you've chosen to abandon your family in this time of need."

Reid bit his tongue. Emotional blackmail? The man had nerve.

Nora scowled. "Is that why you called, Dad? We've been over this. I told you I'd come back if there was a real emergency, but I have myself and my son to take care of. That's the most important thing right now."

Sutton coughed, prolonging the fit past the point where Reid had any concern left. It was clear Winchester was milking it.

When he'd recovered, Sutton glared at Nora. "And where exactly does the Spawn of Satan fit into that, may I ask?" This was the nickname her father had used for Reid ever since discovering that she was spending time with him.

"His name is Reid and you can leave him out of this conversation." Nora's gaze shifted toward Reid, as he stood, crossing behind Nora's chair to rest a hand on her shoulder.

"You rang?" he commented to Winchester mildly.

Reid would be the first in line to agree with the moniker Spawn of Satan. His own father was no doubt in hell trying to dethrone the devil as they spoke. But the fine, pinched lines around Nora's mouth were not okay. Just because she was related to this cruel, miserable man didn't mean Reid would stand by and allow her to be abused.

"Chamberlain," Winchester fairly barked. "Since

warnings to my daughter have gone unheeded, I'll appeal to your sense of honor, whatever little of it you may have. Stay away from Nora. Your bad blood will only lead to pain and suffering. If she won't give you the boot, take it upon yourself to remove yourself from her house."

"Dad, that's enough!" Nora was fairly bristling under Reid's palm. "You have no idea what you're talking about. How dare you intrude on my life and then make demands of a man who's shown me nothing but kindness?"

Kindness? That was laying it on a bit thick but just as Reid was about to tell the old man to go to hell, Winchester cleared his throat. "You're obviously not thinking this through, Nora. You have a son to be concerned with. You do not want him to be negatively affected by your poor choices, do you?"

"The only poor choice I've made lately is making this call," Nora retorted darkly. "And asking this is probably the second one, but I have to know. What, exactly, do you think is going to happen to Declan by being exposed to Reid?"

Nothing good could come of that question, but now that she'd asked, Reid was interested in the answer, too. Not because he had any respect for Winchester's opinion, but simply because Reid had already arrived at the conclusion that he was bad news for mom and son. It couldn't hurt to solidify that fact in both his and Nora's minds.

That the answer came via her father stuck in his craw, though.

"The man is ruthless," Winchester announced as if Reid wasn't standing right there listening. "In his business dealings and his personal relationships, such as they are. Hasn't anyone explained his distasteful reputation to you? He's corrupt, soulless and cold. A man like him cannot be around my grandson. I forbid it."

Hearing it spelled out like that without a filter, without any pulled punches, was brutal. But it didn't make it any less true. He wasn't father material and Winchester saw it as clearly as Reid did.

"Reid," Nora said without turning around. "Tell my father Declan's favorite animal."

"Giraffe." Or at least it was now. He slept with the stuffed giraffe Reid had bought him at the zoo and carried it around as if he'd been gifted with the Hope Diamond.

"What time does he go to bed?"

"Eight o'clock. If you mean for the night. He also takes a nap after lunch." As Reid well knew since he'd taken complete advantage of the all-adult alone time on more than one occasion.

Nora cocked her head at her father, staring him down as she addressed Reid. "What did he eat for breakfast?"

"Cheerios." This was a fun game, especially since Winchester's complexion got grayer and grayer the longer Nora kept it up.

"Now it's your turn, Dad." Nora folded her hands. "If

you can answer at least one of those questions about me from when I was two, I'll take your advice about Reid. Wait, I'll make it even easier. Answer it about me, Eve *or* Grace. Go ahead. Wow me."

Winchester sputtered as Reid's mouth flipped up into an appreciative smile that he didn't bother to hide. God, she was amazing.

"That's what I thought," Nora concluded. "You know how Reid answered those questions so easily? Because he spends time with Declan. He makes an effort. He's already a better father figure to my son than you ever were to me. And you're *my* blood. This conversation is over."

Nora clicked the lid shut to her laptop and put her head down on it.

Reid lightly massaged her shoulders in hopes it would be comforting and tried to unstick his tongue from the roof of his mouth. A *father figure*? That was… What was that? He had no context for the definition of the term, what she'd meant when she'd said it and whether the fifty-pound weight on his chest had landed there because the concept scared him or because it didn't.

After all, he did care about Declan. The kid had grown on him when he wasn't looking. He was funny, innocent and a piece of Nora. What wasn't to like?

Regardless, as far as all those things she'd asked him were concerned, his ability to answer didn't give him any special skill to do something as huge as be a father. Yet Nora seemed to think so or she wouldn't have made that point so well to her own father. Confusion clogged his throat.

"Sorry," she mumbled. "You shouldn't have been subjected to that. I—"

"No problem." This conversation needed some spin control before more things came out of her mouth that tilted his world. "You were brilliant, by the way."

Declan kicked his legs against the plastic footrest of his high chair and said, "Daadee."

And Reid didn't know what he was supposed to do with that, either.

Eleven

That afternoon, Reid tried to shake off the weirdness of the Skype conversation with Sutton Winchester and talked Nora into letting him rent them a sailboat for a spin around Chatfield Reservoir. Nora's small town of Silver Falls lay to the southwest of Denver, right at the foothills of the Rockies, and made for amazing views.

The skyline of Chicago had its own beauty but Reid appreciated the diversity of the vistas here, including the gorgeous blonde at his side as they boarded the fifty-foot cruising sailboat that he'd chartered for their fun afternoon. The captain welcomed them aboard and went over a few safety precautions while Declan explored the small seating area designed for the guests. The captain handed them all orange life vests and Nora actually got

Declan to stand still for four seconds while she strapped him into his. A full crew scurried about the deck, making the sails ready for departure.

The wind kicked up and blew through Nora's hair as they headed out toward the center of the reservoir. It streamed out behind her and she laughed as Declan put his face up to the breeze like a dog sticking his head out the window.

This was the perfect distraction from the heaviness that had weighed Reid down all day. Not that Nora had noticed his reticence, or if she had, she'd elected not to say anything. Maybe she'd been thinking about the conversation, too, wondering if she should take back what she'd told her father. But she hadn't. Probably because she didn't realize that Reid had faulty genetics that prevented him from being the father figure she'd described.

Declan wandered over to the edge of the boat and gripped the railing, watching the water rush by with a happy smile. It jabbed Reid right in the stomach. What a rush to put that kind of expression on a kid's face. The poor guy had it tough with losing his dad and having a sick grandpa. If any of the excursions Reid had planned made his life a little easier, that was fair compensation for how much warmth Declan and Nora had brought to him.

Nora leaned in toward Reid, her eye still on her son. "Thanks for this. It's nice."

He smiled back in response. "Thank you for what you said to your dad."

"You're welcome. You aren't going to argue with me about what I said? I've been waiting for you to bring it up all day."

The seat cushion under Reid's butt grew uncomfortable and he sought a different position. But no amount of fidgeting changed the fact that she was right. He had been avoiding the subject. "You didn't have to say that about me just to get your dad off your back."

"I didn't. It's true." Her hand drifted over to clutch his. "You've been an amazing influence on Declan and he likes you. I know you think you're not father material, but it's obvious to me that you are."

Reid went cold. This was the part where he had to come clean with her. Where he had to be so very clear that answering a few questions about breakfast cereal didn't erase the Chamberlain genes from his makeup. "It's not that I hate the idea of being around kids. Declan is great. It's that I...have a lot of internal stuff to overcome."

"Don't we all?" She dismissed his comment with a wave of her hand. "Besides, I've told you before, I think it's admirable that you stop and think about these things before jumping into the deep end. That's part of what makes you father material, Reid. Because you care so much about doing the right thing. My dad never did. You're already better just in that one respect."

Reid opened his mouth to categorically deny every last word she'd said. And couldn't do it. Because all at once, he got her point. He did care about Declan. And

Nora. How had that happened? He'd have sworn he didn't have the ability to nurture and love, that tragedy had ripped that away from him. Apparently, he'd been wrong. What else had he been wrong about?

He cleared his throat. "Thanks. I'm sorry your father is such a piece of work."

There was so much more he wanted to say but he couldn't get the swirl of emotion in his chest to stop long enough for him to form coherent speech.

"You'd think it would be easier to hate him. But I can't." Nora caught her lip between her front teeth, worrying it as she glanced at Reid. "He's still my father despite all the crappy stuff he's done over the years. Despite the horrible mandates he threw around this morning about you. He's my dad and I still love him. Am I insane?"

"No." He yanked Nora into his arms, simply holding her, because the break in her voice had echoed through the hollow cavity inside his chest and he needed her warmth just then.

He needed *her*.

She'd just described the very essence of unconditional love, something he scarcely understood, but wanted to. Nora had opened up a whole world of possibilities by breathing life into Reid's stale world. By shedding light on all the darkness of his existence. By presenting new ways to view old, set-in-stone beliefs.

If Sutton Winchester had been a horrible excuse for a human being and yet still had managed to retain his daughter's love, perhaps the fatherhood bar wasn't as high as Reid had always assumed it was. Hadn't he been successful at everything he'd ever tried? Why had he always categorically dismissed his weaknesses as bad DNA? Nora had overcome her genetics. She was a great mom. Surely if he tried, he could do leagues better than her father. Or his own.

And if that was true, maybe it wasn't a sin of the highest order to imagine that he'd found something in Nora Winchester O'Malley that was worth hanging on to with both hands—a family. He wanted that.

"I'm glad you're here," she said and pulled back a bit from his embrace. Not all the way, which was fortunate, because he'd just yank her back. "I really didn't expect anything to come out of tracking you down that day after you sent the catering. But I've been carrying this load by myself for so long that I've forgotten how much I need someone to turn to when it gets rough."

Yes, exactly. Her thoughts so eloquently and perfectly mirrored his, it was almost spooky. Or maybe it was just fate.

Hope filled him to the brim and he cleared his throat to tell Nora that something miraculous was happening. Something that afforded them an opportunity to write a different ending to their affair. Grief and darkness had held him back from caring about anyone for so long… and he was sick of being alone. He had an opportunity to be there for Nora and Declan, to perhaps atone for what he'd failed to do for Sophia and his mother.

But at that moment, the winds shifted, billowing the sails backward. The boat lurched as if it had hit a brick wall.

Declan slipped.

Reid watched it happen in slow motion as if time had literally slowed down, allowing him to internalize every second of the little boy's feet sliding out from under him. Declan fell to the deck, his forehead slamming against the wood paneling with a sickening thud. His red curls lay still as the wind died down.

Nora cried out and wobbled to her feet, throwing herself toward the boy. Her hands rushed over her son, checking his crumpled, unmoving form.

Reid's heart jammed into his throat. *No air.* He couldn't move. His hands went numb and useless. He shoved himself off the bench anyway, rushing after Nora to do…something. Anything.

The captain shouted to the crew and the boat settled into the wind. One of the crewmembers knelt by Declan and spoke to Nora, gently checking the boy's pulse.

The crewmember motioned Reid out of the way, so he crouched on the opposite side to smooth a hand over Nora's back because he needed to do something and this was the best spot to monitor the situation. Someone had to make sure Declan was being taken care of and it should be Reid since he was responsible for the injury.

Blood smeared Declan's forehead. The crewmember asked Nora's permission to hold a bandage on it, explaining the risks of concussion as tears streamed down Nora's face unchecked.

Reid's gut clenched. This was all his fault. Declan was too young to be out on a boat this size. A real father would have known that. Would have known what to do when his kid was hurt. But Reid didn't because he wasn't Declan's father. Nor should he be.

Sutton Winchester could see Reid's unsuitability a mile away. Like recognized like in the end. Perhaps Nora had completely missed the point of her father's warning. Instead of resisting it, she should have realized her father had in fact only been looking out for her because he'd be gone soon and unable to do so any longer. In a way, it was a complete reversal of Winchester's typical method of operation.

And the old man's point hadn't been lost on Reid. If Nora wouldn't listen to reason, then Reid had to be the one to do the right thing. The thing he'd known would be the end result of this affair all along—he had to extract himself from Nora and Declan's world before he hurt them even more. Because he loved them both.

The boat butted up against the dock. An ambulance sat idling nearby and two EMTs in dark blue uniforms stood on the dock waiting until the boat was secured. The instant the ropes held, they clambered on board and went to work evaluating Declan.

Nora's gaze never left her son. As well it shouldn't. Though Reid felt her slipping away even as he made conscious effort to let her go. In reality, she'd never been his and he'd never had any kind of claim on her. So whatever connection he'd become so aware of, so dependent on, couldn't continue.

The EMTs explained that only family could ride in the ambulance to the hospital and Nora nodded, finally glancing at Reid as if she'd just realized he was there. The look on her face—ravaged, tear-stained—gutted him. He'd done that to her, caused her pain and worry for her son by being so clueless about safety.

He had reasons why he didn't know more about kids. But they weren't good ones. And definitely not excuses. When you didn't know something and it was important to learn, you learned. Why hadn't he done that?

Because he'd been trying to turn his brief affair with Nora into something meaningful to assuage his own loneliness. He was nothing if not self-serving.

It was time to change that.

"I'm sorry, Reid," she murmured, her voice just as ravaged as her face. "I'm going to ride in the ambulance with Declan, but they're saying you'll have to take separate transportation. I can't… Well, I have to go."

He nodded. "No problem. You do whatever you need to do."

Separating from Nora and Declan was perfect for his purposes, actually. He watched the EMTs load the still-unconscious boy onto the gurney and then roll it into the back of the waiting ambulance. He helped Nora into the cavernous space and squeezed her hand one final time before the driver shut the door. Then the ambulance drove away, taking with it the only people who had managed to coax a smile out of Reid in a very long time.

The oil slick in his soul bubbled up, crowding out all the good waking up with Nora this morning had done. He shouldn't have come here and allowed the darkness that lived inside him to harm others. And he surely shouldn't have bribed Nora with a private plane ride here in order to stay in her orbit. Because he selfishly wanted a family without giving anything of himself.

Easily fixed. He'd just leave his pilot and plane here and fly back to Chicago some other way. The trick would be not letting on to Nora how much it hurt to not be the man she deserved and the father Declan deserved.

Reid hadn't come to the hospital and Nora had a pretty good idea why. Exhausted, Nora pushed open the front door of her house with one hand and shifted a sleeping Declan higher against her hip, making sure she didn't jostle his brand-new stitches.

"Reid," she called softly and shook her head when he didn't answer. The man was a big, fat scaredy-cat and he needed to see with his own two eyes that Declan was fine. Which wouldn't happen if he kept hiding away from the frightening parts of life.

It was a step back. A small one. Slowly but surely, Reid had been coming around to the idea that kids weren't all that bad and then this had to happen. A bump on the head that would heal in time. Like all wounds.

She'd thought maybe Reid had gotten to a place where he believed that. Where they could really talk to each other about their fears and setbacks, and yeah, maybe share in the triumphs.

She could have used his strong shoulder at the hospital. She was a little upset that he hadn't realized that.

First things first. She got Declan undressed and in his crib with his stuffed giraffe, then covered him with his frog blanket. The boy didn't stir, likely a combination of the late hour and the activity at the hospital. Then she went in search of Reid.

The house was dark and silent. Reid wasn't here.

Frowning, she glanced around her bedroom and immediately noted his suitcases were gone. In the kitchen, she found a handwritten note, folded, with her name on the outside.

Her stomach sank as she picked up the page. The flowing script blurred as she took in the contents. Apparently, it didn't take many lines to rip her heart out.

One, two, three... She let the pain take over until she reached ten. Then she cut it off.

He was gone. Without explanation. "It's my fault Declan was hurt. It's better we end things now before something worse happens," was *not* an explanation.

Anger bloomed, hot and fierce. That...*man*. How dare he leave her when she needed him most? She'd kept her panic and tears under control while watching the doctor stitch up her baby, but only because she'd had to. It didn't stop her from wishing Reid had been there to hold her in the hallway while she crumbled. She was so tired of not being able to crumble, of not having someone strong enough to catch her.

Why did she always have to fall for men who were determined to leave? First she'd fallen for a man with such deep wanderlust, he'd enlisted in the army to satisfy it. And he'd paid the ultimate price with his life. She didn't begrudge Sean his choices, nor blame him for dying, but she did wish she'd had an opportunity to say goodbye. It was her biggest unresolvable regret.

As for Reid, she could blame him all day long for his choices. Jetting off and leaving her a note. That was... unforgivable. And all at once, she didn't plan to stand for it. Sean had left her to go to a place she couldn't follow. But Reid hadn't.

The note indicated that Reid had left his plane at the private airstrip not far from Silver Falls, which was available for her use to return to Chicago whenever she deemed it necessary.

It looked as though that time was now.

In the morning, she threw the load of laundry from the dryer back into the same suitcases the clothes had come from yesterday and zipped them up. Declan was a bit harder to herd as he was still tired and cranky from the bump on his head. But she prevailed and Reid's pilot took off for Chicago before lunchtime.

After an uneventful flight where Nora passed the time fuming over Reid's cowardice, she made a quick call to Grace, who dropped everything in order to take

Declan. This was one showdown that didn't need an additional audience member.

Finally, Nora walked through the door of the Metropol business office and faced down Reid's admin. "I'm here to see Mr. Chamberlain. He's expecting me."

It wasn't a lie. He should be expecting her. If he thought she was going to take that BS note at face value, he had another think coming.

"Oh." Reid's admin's eyes rounded. "Yes, you should definitely go right in."

Nora was all too happy to comply, but when she stormed into Reid's office, the genuine shock on his face when he looked up from his desk brought her up short.

The force of his presence slammed into her, far more powerfully than it had the first time she'd come here. His brown eyes were full of secret pain and even more secret longing. His body, as she knew firsthand, was full of heat and tenderness. And her heart was full of him.

They'd come full circle. A few weeks ago, she'd been looking for an old friend. Today, she was looking for the man she'd fallen in love with. And had only just realized that was the root of her anger.

She loved Reid. How dare he treat that so casually? Didn't he realize how hard it was for her to open her heart again? How afraid she was of loss?

Her legs started shaking but she shrugged her nervousness off, marching forward to yank the phone out of Reid's hand.

"He'll have to call you back," she said and ended

the call, tossing the phone over her shoulder. "You left. That note? Not going to cut it. Tell me to my face that we're through and I might believe you. But I don't think you can do it. Because you know we're not even close to finished."

"Nora." Reid's gaze swept over her hungrily, weakening her already-shaking legs. "What are you doing here? Is Declan okay? Or is it your father?"

"No, nothing's changed with my father's health and Declan is fine. I just told you why I'm here." Something broke inside as he stood, circling the desk to invade her space, drawing close, so close. But not close enough. There was an invisible barrier between them that she ached to destroy but first, she had to understand. "I deserve to hear from you personally what's going on in your head. We're not just sleeping together. We're involved, whether you like it or not. I thought…"

All at once, as his expression darkened with something she had no idea how to interpret, she faltered. What *had* she thought? That Reid accompanying her to Colorado meant something different from what it had? That he'd turned into someone who wanted a woman with a kid? His refusal to entertain the idea of ever becoming a father couldn't have been clearer. When she'd gently tried to help him see that he'd surely be a better father than most, he hadn't agreed with her. And he hadn't come to the hospital because that was too much for him to handle.

She'd run all the way back to Chicago to confront a

man who wanted out from their affair. She should have left well enough alone.

"You thought what?" His voice dipped dangerously low. "That something was happening between us? That I might have developed feelings for you?"

"Yes." She couldn't look away. Couldn't lie. Even though she knew it was the wrong tactic, the absolute worst thing to admit to a man who had run away from her as fast as he could. The facts spoke for themselves after all. "Tell me I'm wrong. Say it. Out loud."

"You're not." The phrase reverberated in the air, settling across her skin. Raising goose bumps as his eyes bored into her. "That's why I left. Because I care about you too much to hurt you."

"What are you saying?" she whispered as everything inside her slid off a cliff. "You…left because you developed feelings for me?"

"I can't…" He shook his head. "That's why I left the note. It was supposed to keep you in Colorado. Where you were safe. Not drag you back to Chicago. Go home. I'm not good for you."

"Reid." His name bubbled up on a sob as she fought back tears. "That's ridiculous. You're the best thing that's happened to me in a long, dark couple of years. I need you. And you left. *That's* what hurt."

His gaze was raw as he nearly closed the gap between them. But didn't. "I'm sorry. I was trying to protect Declan. And you. I've caused enough pain."

"Protect us from what? You?" She tried to laugh it

off but the sound got caught in her throat. "Declan is fine. Kids get hurt. They're not as fragile as you seem to think. But I don't buy that as the reason for all of this. I think you ran because of what's happening between us."

To her shock, he nodded. "Yes. Because it's the right thing to do. I never expected to fall for you and never expected to have to make the difficult choice to walk away."

She nearly groaned at the irony. The one time he'd elected to make an adult decision, and it was the wrong one. "Then don't walk away. Seize the moment. And the next one. For the next fifty or sixty years, let's be crazy together. I love you and I'm not leaving until you say yes."

To emphasize the point, she plopped down on his desk, crossing her arms. Nora Winchester O'Malley charted her own destiny and she wanted this man, with all his glorious complexities.

She wasn't leaving without his heart.

He hesitated for an eternity and then his fingers slid around her elbows, pulling her to her feet. For a half second, she thought he was going to throw her out. But then he swept her into his arms, kissing her with an intensity she could scarcely take in.

His essence swirled into her soul, joining them in a connection that couldn't be explained but didn't have to be. Because they both felt it. Both yearned for it. Both accepted it, despite all their objections to the contrary.

When he finally let her surface long enough to gulp

in some much-needed oxygen, he murmured, "I'm sorry. I shouldn't have done that. It's not fair to keep drawing you back in. You should leave."

"No." She scowled. "And I'm not letting you make this decision for me. I want you in my life. And in Declan's. We both need you."

He pierced her with his deep, soulful eyes. "I don't know how to be a father. What if there's something wrong with me that I can't overcome? You're taking too big of a chance with your son on what's essentially a work in progress."

Even now, he was trying so hard to do the right thing and couldn't see that she accepted him as he was. "Since we're on the subject, I'm a work in progress, too. I know everything about being a mom of a one-year-old. But I've never been the mom of a two-year-old. It's a lot harder. I'm making all new mistakes. That's where you come in. Be there for me. As my sounding board. As my lover, to help the bad parts of the day melt away. As my partner. That, you know how to do."

Because he'd been doing it all along. And she'd been too blind to see that she needed to encourage it, nurture their blossoming relationship by telling him every moment how important he was to her.

"Guess we know where Declan gets his stubbornness from. Seems like his mom latches on to an idea and never lets go, either."

"I don't know what you're talking about," she countered primly, her pulse racing to keep up with all the things going on inside. "I'm not stubborn. I just know what I want. And you, Reid Chamberlain, are it."

He shook his head and her heart froze. But then he smiled, the real genuine one that made her feel like she'd won the Reid Chamberlain sweepstakes and everything was going to be all right.

"What if I just want to be friends?" he asked, even as his arms slid around her, possessively, intimately, drawing her so close there was nothing between them.

Everything inside yearned for this man. "Too bad. You better get used to the idea of being lovers *and* friends. And one last thing. No more notes."

His lips toyed with hers, not quite completing the connection. "Not even 'I love you' scrawled in the steam on the bathroom mirror?"

She pretended to contemplate it but the thought of sharing a bathroom with Reid for the rest of her life made her a little giddy. "That one might be okay. But only if you promise to follow it up verbally."

"I do."

The sweetest words in the English language. "Then so do I."

Epilogue

Nora hid a smile as Reid picked up Declan and hoisted him to his shoulders, then galloped around the living area of his Metropol penthouse. The neighing noises Reid was making were her favorite. It was the kind of thing Reid did frequently without thought and Nora fell a little more in love with the man every time he came up with a new game to play with her son.

And soon, Declan would be Reid's son, too. They'd already filed adoption papers.

Reid had put Chamberlain Group on the back burner in favor of learning everything he could about being a father, claiming he had to catch up fast. Before it became official. He didn't seem to understand it had been official since the moment Declan had picked Reid as his "Daadee."

Nora's phone rang and she scooped it up when she saw Grace's name on the screen.

"Everything okay?" Nora asked anxiously. Every phone call from a family member could be the one where she got word that her father had died. When Dr. Wilde had given Sutton Winchester until New Year's to live, it didn't necessarily mean he'd make it until then.

Before Reid and Nora had gotten married, they'd agreed to split their time between Chicago and Silver Falls, at least until the first of the year. Eventually, they hoped to buy a bigger house higher up in the foothills of the Rockies, one that would accommodate the brood of children they both wanted. But for now, Chicago was where Nora needed to be.

"No, everything is not okay," Grace said. Nora could hear the scowl in her sister's voice. "You are not going to believe what those Newport scum have done now."

The call wasn't about her father. Nora breathed a sigh of relief and wandered into the kitchen to sit at the island. "Brooks and Graham? What have they done?"

More inheritance drama. But that came part and parcel with being a Winchester. Nora's patience with it had grown the longer she had Reid to lean on.

And when leaning on his strong shoulder wasn't enough, he just took her to bed and made love to her until she forgot about everything outside of the two of them.

Grace made a very uncomplimentary noise. "They

hired a private investigator to work with that lawyer, Josh Calhoun."

"They went ahead with involving their friend in this?" Nora's stomach sank. The Newport twins were fired up about getting Carson his share of the Winchester fortune and honestly, she didn't get their passion for the quest. "I don't understand what a private investigator is going to add to the mix other than making more of a mess."

"Yeah. They want to find their real father, and I guess a private investigator is supposed to help with that. But I didn't tell you the worst part. The PI is Roman Slater." Grace nearly spat out the name. "My ex."

"Oh, Grace." Nora still remembered how her sister had cried for the six months following her breakup with Roman. "I can't believe they would stoop to working with someone so underhanded."

The twins were obviously trouble waiting to happen, and must have been deliberately involving people they thought were going to put the screws to the Winchesters. It was unforgivable.

"Well, Dad is being so closemouthed about their parentage. I'm even starting to believe he knows something."

Nora secretly agreed. Since moving into Reid's penthouse, she'd tried to spend at least three days a week at the hospital and really talk to her father. Amazingly, her dad had completely reversed his stance on Reid with no explanation, only stating—very gruffly—that he'd heard Reid had appointed Nash as the interim CEO of Chamberlain Group while he spent time with his new family. Sutton approved.

None of it made up for the years of not having a father. But Nora was slowly letting go of her disappointment and grief. Reid's love helped with that, too. When her father finally passed, she felt more confident than ever that she would be at peace with it.

"I'm glad you're here, Nora," Gracie admitted. "I have a feeling this whole thing is going to get uglier before long."

"Yeah, me, too. Sorry. Let me know what I can do to help."

Nora disconnected the call and returned to the living room to find Reid and Declan in the middle of the floor, laughing so hard, neither of them could breathe. Her soul filled with the sound. How had she gotten so lucky to find a man who could love her son as much as she did?

"What's all of this?" Nora demanded. "Having fun without me?"

"Never," Reid said, his gorgeous grin spreading across his face. "Care to join us, Ms. O'Malley?"

He smiled all the time these days and she delighted in taking full credit for it.

"That's Mrs. Chamberlain to you, buddy," she corrected and the sound of her new name thrilled her. She'd sworn to never change her name again, but that was before she found it vitally necessary to be joined with this man in every way possible.

He was her friend. Her lover. Her husband. Soon to be the legal father of her child. And she would never let him go.

* * * * *

Don't miss a single installment of
DYNASTIES: THE NEWPORTS
Passion and chaos consume a
Chicago real estate empire

SAYING YES TO THE BOSS by Andrea Laurence
AN HEIR FOR THE BILLIONAIRE by Kat Cantrell
CLAIMED BY THE COWBOY by Sarah M. Anderson
HIS SECRET BABY BOMBSHELL by Jules Bennett
BACK IN THE ENEMY'S BED by Michelle Celmer
THE TEXAN'S ONE NIGHT STAND-OFF
by Charlene Sands

Available now from Harlequin Desire!

COMING NEXT MONTH FROM

HARLEQUIN®
Desire

Available September 6, 2016

#2467 THE RANCHER'S ONE-WEEK WIFE
by Kathie DeNosky

Wealthy rancher Blake and city-girl Karly's whirlwind rodeo romance ends with wedding vows—and then reality sets in! But during the delivery of divorce papers, she's stranded at his ranch. Can they turn their one week into forever?

#2468 THE BOSS'S BABY ARRANGEMENT
Billionaires and Babies • by Catherine Mann

A marriage of convenience between an executive single dad and his sexy employee in need of a green card *should* have nothing to do with passion...but their carefully laid plan goes out the window when their hearts become involved!

#2469 EXPECTING HIS SECRET HEIR
Mill Town Millionaires • by Dani Wade

Mission: dig up dirt on Zach Gatlin, so he'll be disqualified from inheriting the fortune he doesn't know exists. Payment: enough money to cover Sadie's critically ill sister's medical bills. Approach: seduction. Complication: her heart...and a baby!

#2470 CLAIMED BY THE COWBOY
Dynasties: The Newports • by Sarah M. Anderson

Cowboy Josh Calhoun is only in Chicago to help a friend, but he unexpectedly gets a second chance with Dr. Lucinda Wilde. He let her go once out of respect for his best friend, but this time he plans to claim her...

#2471 BILLIONAIRE BOSS, M.D.
The Billionaires of Black Castle • by Olivia Gates

As her new boss, billionaire doctor Antonio Balducci plans to use medical researcher Liliana Accardi to destroy those who left him to a hellish fate. But when love unexpectedly overwhelms him, could it overcome his need for vengeance?

#2472 SECOND CHANCE WITH THE CEO
The Serenghetti Brothers • by Anna DePalo

Beautiful Marisa Danieli is the reason former athlete turned CEO Cole Serenghetti missed a major career goal, something he's never forgotten—or forgiven. How unfortunate for her that the sexy tycoon is the one thing standing between her and the promotion she needs...

YOU CAN FIND MORE INFORMATION ON UPCOMING HARLEQUIN® TITLES, FREE EXCERPTS AND MORE AT WWW.HARLEQUIN.COM.

HDCNM0816

REQUEST YOUR FREE BOOKS!
2 FREE NOVELS PLUS 2 FREE GIFTS!

ALWAYS POWERFUL, PASSIONATE AND PROVOCATIVE

YES! Please send me 2 FREE Harlequin® Desire novels and my 2 FREE gifts (gifts are worth about $10). After receiving them, if I don't wish to receive any more books, I can return the shipping statement marked "cancel." If I don't cancel, I will receive 6 brand-new novels every month and be billed just $4.55 per book in the U.S. or $5.24 per book in Canada. That's a savings of at least 13% off the cover price! It's quite a bargain! Shipping and handling is just 50¢ per book in the U.S. and 75¢ per book in Canada.* I understand that accepting the 2 free books and gifts places me under no obligation to buy anything. I can always return a shipment and cancel at any time. Even if I never buy another book, the two free books and gifts are mine to keep forever.

225/326 HDN GH2P

Name	(PLEASE PRINT)	
Address		Apt. #
City	State/Prov.	Zip/Postal Code

Signature (if under 18, a parent or guardian must sign)

Mail to the **Reader Service:**

IN U.S.A.: P.O. Box 1867, Buffalo, NY 14240-1867
IN CANADA: P.O. Box 609, Fort Erie, Ontario L2A 5X3

Want to try two free books from another line?
Call 1-800-873-8635 or visit www.ReaderService.com.

* Terms and prices subject to change without notice. Prices do not include applicable taxes. Sales tax applicable in N.Y. Canadian residents will be charged applicable taxes. Offer not valid in Quebec. This offer is limited to one order per household. Not valid for current subscribers to Harlequin Desire books. All orders subject to credit approval. Credit or debit balances in a customer's account(s) may be offset by any other outstanding balance owed by or to the customer. Please allow 4 to 6 weeks for delivery. Offer available while quantities last.

Your Privacy—The Reader Service is committed to protecting your privacy. Our Privacy Policy is available online at www.ReaderService.com or upon request from the Reader Service.

We make a portion of our mailing list available to reputable third parties that offer products we believe may interest you. If you prefer that we not exchange your name with third parties, or if you wish to clarify or modify your communication preferences, please visit us at www.ReaderService.com/consumerschoice or write to us at Reader Service Preference Service, P.O. Box 9062, Buffalo, NY 14240-9062. Include your complete name and address.

HDI5

SPECIAL EXCERPT FROM

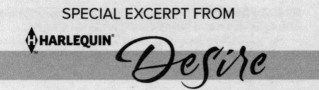
HARLEQUIN

Desire

*A marriage of convenience between an executive single
dad and his sexy employee in need of a green card
should have nothing to do with passion...but their
carefully laid plan goes out the window when their
hearts become involved!*

Read on for a sneak peek at
THE BOSS'S BABY ARRANGEMENT,
by USA TODAY *bestselling author*
Catherine Mann
and part of the bestselling
BILLIONAIRES AND BABIES *series.*

Maureen Burke danced with abandon.

Throwing herself into this pocket of time, matching the
steps of this leanly athletic man with charismatic blue eyes and
a sexual intensity as potent as his handsome face.

Brains. Brilliance. A body to die for and a loyal love of
family.

Xander Lourdes was a good man.

But not her man.

So Maureen allowed herself to dance with the abandon she
never would have dared otherwise. Not now. Not after all she'd
been through.

She allowed herself to be swept away by the dance, the
music and the pulse of the drums pushing through her veins
with every heartbeat, faster and faster. Arching timbres of the
steel drums urged her to absorb every fiber of this moment.

Too soon, her work visa was due to expire, and officials had
thus far denied her requests to extend it. She would have to go

home. To face all she'd run from, to leave this amazing place where abandon meant beauty and exuberance. Freedom.

She was free to look now, though, at this man with coal-black hair that spiked with the sea breeze and a hint of sweat. His square jaw was peppered with a five-o'clock shadow, his shoulders broad in his tuxedo, broad enough to carry the weight of the world.

Shivering with warm tingles that had nothing to do with any bonfire or humid night, she could feel the attraction radiating off him the same way it heated in her. She'd sensed the draw before but his grief was so well-known she hadn't wanted to wade into those complicated waters. But with her return to home looming...

Maureen wasn't interested in a relationship, but maybe if she was leaving she could indulge in—

Suddenly his attention was yanked from her. He reached into his tuxedo pocket and pulled out his cell phone and read the text.

Tension pulsed through his jaw, the once-relaxed, half-cocked smile replaced instantly with a serious expression. "It's the nanny. My daughter's running a fever. I have to go."

And without another word, he was gone and she knew she was gone from his thoughts. That little girl was the world to him. Everyone knew that as well as how deeply he grieved for his dead wife.

All of which merely made him more attractive.

More dangerous to her peace of mind.

Don't miss THE BOSS'S BABY ARRANGEMENT
by USA TODAY bestselling author Catherine Mann.
available September 2016 wherever
Harlequin® Desire books and ebooks are sold.

If you enjoyed this excerpt, pick up a new
BILLIONAIRES AND BABIES *book every month!*

It's the #1 bestselling series from Harlequin® Desire—
Powerful men...wrapped around their babies' little fingers.

www.Harlequin.com

Copyright © 2016 by Catherine Mann

HDEXP0816

Whatever You're Into… Passionate Reads

Looking for more passionate reads from Harlequin®?
Fear not! Harlequin® Presents, Harlequin® Desire and
Harlequin® Blaze offer you irresistible romance stories
featuring powerful heroes.

HARLEQUIN *Presents*

Do you want alpha males, decadent glamour and jet-set
lifestyles? Step into the sensational, sophisticated world of
Harlequin® Presents, where sinfully tempting heroes ignite a
fierce and wickedly irresistible passion!

HARLEQUIN *Desire*

Harlequin® Desire novels are powerful, passionate and
provocative contemporary romances set against a backdrop of
wealth, privilege and sweeping family saga. Alpha heroes with
a soft side meet strong-willed but vulnerable heroines amid a
dramatic world of divided loyalties, high-stakes conflict and
intense emotion.

HARLEQUIN *Blaze*

Harlequin® Blaze stories sizzle with strong heroines and
irresistible heroes playing the game of modern love and lust.
They're fun, sexy and always steamy.

Be sure to check out our full selection of books
within each series every month!

www.Harlequin.com

HPASSION2016

**Join for FREE today at
www.HarlequinMyRewards.com**

Earn **FREE BOOKS** of your choice.

Experience **EXCLUSIVE OFFERS** and contests.

Enjoy **BOOK RECOMMENDATIONS**
selected just for you.

PLUS! Sign up now
and get **500** points
right away!

MYR16R

HARLEQUIN®

A Romance FOR EVERY MOOD™

Love the Harlequin book
you just read?

Your opinion matters.

Review this book on your favorite
book site, review site, blog or your own
social media properties and share
your opinion with other readers!

Be sure to connect with us at:
Harlequin.com/Newsletters
Facebook.com/HarlequinBooks
Twitter.com/HarlequinBooks